Contents

1. ARABELLA — 1
2. MATTEO — 10
3. ARABELLA — 18
4. MATTEO — 26
5. ARABELLA — 35
6. MATTEO — 44
7. ARABELLA — 53
8. MATTEO — 62
9. ARABELLA — 71
10. MATTEO — 79
11. ARABELLA — 88
12. MATTEO — 96
13. ARABELLA — 104
14. MATTEO — 113

15. ARABELLA 121
16. MATTEO 129
17. ARABELLA 137
18. MATTEO 145
19. ARABELLA 153
20. MATTEO 161
21. EPILOGUE 166
22. BLURB 170

Shielded By The Mafia Boss

A Billionaire Secret Baby Romance

Bobbie Quinn

Copyright © Oct 2023, by Bobbie Quinn.

All rights reserved.

No portion of this book may be reproduced in any form without written permission from the publisher or author, except as permitted by U.S. copyright law.

Chapter 1

ARABELLA

"These are the Arego files. I need the Arego 2 files. Could you at least try to get it right?"

Matteo Romano wasn't the worst billionaire in New York City to work for, but he wasn't the best either. He was abrupt, cold, and stern. He never said please or thank you, and I swear he still hadn't learned my name, even though I'd been working for him for three weeks.

Still, I was lucky to be his personal assistant. It was a great job at one of the biggest tech companies in America and far away enough from my father that I didn't have to worry about him being involved in my life anymore.

"Here you go, sir," I said as I handed the files over to my boss, managing to keep my tone polite even though I was sure he'd asked for the wrong files in the first place.

"Coffee, black and no sugar" was all I got back. I'd made him approximately 100 cups of coffee since I'd started working for him, so I couldn't understand why he kept telling me how he took it. It was like he thought I didn't have a single working brain cell.

I made my way to the executive breakroom to get him his coffee (black, no sugar) and nearly walked directly into another assistant.

"Sorry, sorry, sorry." The short brunette apologized repeatedly as she grabbed the milk from the fridge. "Carlyle will have my head if he doesn't get his cappuccino in the next five minutes."

"No worries. I get it. Mr. Romano is equally as demanding. I'm Arabella, by the way."

I hadn't made friends with the other assistants yet, and I really wanted some workplace allies.

"Oh shit, you're Romano's latest assistant? You've got it rough. That man, as deliciously hot as he is, is a cold one. I don't think I've ever seen him smile. Oh, and my name's Debbie."

She stuck out one hand for me to shake while she held the milk.

"Better get Carlyle his caffeine. It was nice to meet you. Join us for lunch sometime."

Before I could answer, she was out the door, almost running to her boss' office.

She seemed nice enough, if not a little rushed. I took my time with the complicated coffee machine, not in a hurry to get back to Mr. Romano's glacial attitude. The executive breakroom was not so much for the executives but rather for their assistants. It's where we stored their weird green juices, milk of every kind, and imported coffee beans. The fridge was filled with fancy foods, even though most of the executives at Gallbury Tech ate lunch out or had it delivered.

"Did you grow the beans yourself?" My delightful boss asked without looking up as I placed his coffee on the table.

I took a deep breath and plastered a smile on my face. There was no point in losing this job because I couldn't take a little sarcasm. I'd grown up with a lot worse. Speaking of "a lot worse", I took a peek at my phone to see that I had another three missed calls from a strange number.

I knew exactly who it was, but I wasn't going to give in. I hadn't spoken to my father in six months, and I didn't intend to break that winning streak. Liam Flynn had never been the bearer of good news in all 57 years of his life.

"Am I keeping you from something, Miss Flynn?" I looked up to see my boss' intense brown eyes staring coldly at me.

"No, sir, I was just checking the time." It took everything I had to sound pleasant rather than sarcastic.

"Perhaps you should consider purchasing a watch. Then you won't be so distracted by your phone during the workday."

"Not all of us have money to burn." *Shit, shit, shit.* I hadn't meant to say that out loud, let alone snap at the man paying my salary.

"Excuse me? I didn't quite get that?" His voice was stern, but I could swear there was a hint of a smile.

"I'm going to run out for lunch now if that's okay with you?" I needed to get out of there as fast as humanly possible.

I swear I heard him mutter, "Run, little rabbit, run", as I swiftly exited his office. I struggled against the urge to show him my middle finger as I fled. *I need this job*, I repeatedly reminded myself.

Instead of leaving the building altogether to find a suitable lunch place, I decided to check out the Gallbury Tech cafeteria and see what was being served. I'd heard good things, but I hadn't really wanted to sit alone in a room full of people since starting at the company. But I wasn't going to make any friends if I kept to myself, was I?

I picked up a smoked salmon salad, an iced Chai latte, and a couple of chocolate chip cookies (which I slipped into my handbag). I looked around for a place to pay but couldn't see anything resembling a till.

"It's all free."

I turned around and spotted Debbie from the executive breakroom standing behind me.

"Really?"

"Yeah, it's one of the perks of working here. Sometimes, I take an extra portion for home so I don't have to bother cooking dinner."

"If I'd known that sooner, it wouldn't have taken me so long to come here."

"Well, now that you are here, you have to join us." Debbie pointed at a table with three other women, ranging from early twenties to late thirties.

I didn't hesitate. Given my boss's tendency to be cold and cruel, I needed some friends at Gallbury Tech, and it wasn't going to be any of the executives who pretended their assistants didn't exist until they needed something.

Debbie introduced me to the other personal assistants. Trudy was the one with gorgeous bright red hair, Donna was a slight and small blonde woman, and Hannah was an eternally smiling brunette who towered over the rest of us... and I was by no means short.

Lunch was a happy, fun little moment out of my day, and I was sad when it was over. I didn't have many friends in New York. In fact, I only had one if I had to be honest. I loved Brian, but unless I ventured into the bright and bustling gay bar where he worked, I didn't get a lot of face time with him.

We'd met when I'd been confused between our two doors and tried to get into his apartment, which was a floor before mine. I'd been in near hysterics - new to the city and a little flustered - when the key wouldn't work. He opened up the door, half asleep, and invited me inside for a margarita. We'd been friends ever since.

I was sad when lunch was over and needed to return to my desk right outside the terrifying Mr. Romano's office. Don't get me wrong, I didn't hate my job. In fact, working at a company like Gallbury Tech in the Big Apple was the kind of thing my dreams were made of. I just wished that my boss was a little less of a tyrant.

As I walked over to my desk, I noticed a shiny black box. I immediately assumed that someone wanted to give Mr. Romano something but was too afraid to disturb him, so they decided to make it my job instead. Then I noticed the note on top of the box.

"Miss Flynn, now you have a watch."

I opened the box and saw the most beautiful rose gold watch with a mother of pearl face. I didn't recognize the brand, which led me to assume that it was beyond my salary bracket. It was absolutely gorgeous. I had to stop myself from grinning ear to ear.

I couldn't accept a gift like this. Not from my cold and distant boss. It didn't make sense. He shouldn't be spending his lunch break purchasing me a watch. He would have had to go out and get it himself because I was usually the person sent to buy gifts.

I walked into his office with every intention of giving him the watch back and promising to purchase my own, more affordable version.

"Yes, you can accept it. No, I will not take it back. It's a fucking watch. Don't make a big deal out of it, Miss Flynn."

He didn't even look up. I simply turned and walked back to my desk. I didn't have a comeback. I was used to standing up to powerful men; I'd been doing it my whole life. But for some reason, Mr. Romano's kindness left me feeling strange. I couldn't find the words to fight back. Probably because I really loved the watch.

I spent the next few hours doing general admin for my boss. It wasn't challenging work, but I didn't mind. It meant that I got to live in New York City and support myself. So many of the girls I'd grown up with relied on the men in their lives for everything, including my own sister. And believe me, the boys we'd grown up around weren't good people.

For as long as I could remember, I'd been brought up around tough men. My father worked for the Irish mob, and the guys were always around, drinking and causing trouble. My mother passed away when I was only eight years old, and after that, Father didn't care about much except his work, beer, and whiskey.

I stole a glance at my phone, noting the seven missed calls from an unknown number. I'd have to speak to my father at some point. If I ignored him long enough, he'd send someone from Boston to see me in person. That's what men like him did: they didn't take no for an answer.

I decided that once Mr. Romano left for the day, I'd tidy his office up and then call the number back. I didn't want to do it at home; it made me feel too vulnerable. At least, at work, it wouldn't feel like he was in my personal space.

Tidying my boss's office wasn't part of my job description, but I hated messes, and that man left his office in disarray every single night. Technically, I finished at five pm, but usually, I walked out as late as eight. It wasn't too much of an issue as I didn't have anywhere to go unless Brian was in the mood to hang out.

I needed to make more friends. Eventually, I was alone in the office, aside from the cleaners. I went into the stairwell and called the unknown number, knowing it would be Father who answered.

"Ari, you should know better than to ignore me."

"What do you want?"

I tried as best I could to keep my voice from shaking.

"You need to come home now. You've had your fun being a city girl, but you've got a responsibility to your family."

"And what exactly do you mean by that?"

"I've made a deal with Ronan Sullivan. You're to marry his son, Cullen. I don't want any shit from you. It's been decided, and you know what will happen if you disobey. If you're not home by next week, I'll have someone come get you…and they won't be as kind as me."

And with that, he hung up. He never let me speak. Liam Flynn believed that women were there to serve the men in their lives and not talk back.

"Shit."

The tears didn't start to flow immediately. Instead, I sat there in stunned silence. I knew exactly who Cullen Sullivan was. We'd grown up in the same circles. His father was the head of the mob, and Cullen was bred to follow in his footsteps. From what I'd seen, he was a cruel man who treated women with the same disdain as men like Father did.

Then, the tears started falling.

Chapter 2
MATTEO

"Matteo, what do you think? Should we wait for their next shipment to arrive or strike the warehouse now?"

"If we really want to send a message, it's best to be patient. Right now, they have very little to lose. If we wait until the shipment has been delivered, we could hit them where it hurts the most."

I didn't really care whether we hit the Russians now or later, but Father was looking to me to contribute. It was his dream that I take his place as the head of the Romano family once he decided to retire. My brother was more than willing, but I was the eldest, and, traditionally, it was the eldest son that took over.

I was far more interested in my position as CEO of Gallbury Tech, but you didn't just leave the mafia. That wasn't how things worked in our world. I loved and respected my father and was, therefore, willing to remain a part of the Romano family business. But I would have to break it to him one day that I didn't want the top job.

"It is decided then: we hit them when it hurts the most."

I nodded at Father, drained the last sip of scotch from my glass, and stood up. We were situated in the back room of my uncle's old-school Italian restaurant. Was it a cliche? Yes, probably. But it gave us the privacy we needed to do business without having people coming in and out of our homes. They also made a killer carbonara.

"Where are you off to, Matteo?"

My aunt cleared my place and tried to get me to sit down again. I knew exactly what she was getting at. That woman couldn't stand the idea of me leaving before dessert. But if I ate her tiramisu every time I visited, I wouldn't fit into my seat anymore.

"I've got to get back to the office. We've been working on a new product feature, and it's been giving everyone a bit of a headache."

"Honestly, Matteo, why do you bother with all that? You have a job right here. You don't need to be going into an office every day. You want money? We can give it to you. You want power? We can give you that too. Everything you could dream of, you have right here."

"Goodnight, everyone, have a good one."

I didn't bother responding to Father. He knew how important Gallbury Tech was to me. I'd started the business back in high school with just my computer and a few cups of coffee. While he didn't necessarily understand having a life outside the family, that didn't mean he didn't respect my decisions.

When I got back to the office, it was just past nine pm. I took the stairs as I usually did. It helped clear my head, and get me pumped up and ready to work. By the time I reached the second floor, I could hear faint sobs coming from the floor above. I raced up the next couple of flights to find out what the hell was happening. No one except the cleaning crew was usually there that late.

When I reached the fourth floor, I saw my assistant sitting on the top stair, her head in her hands.

Fuck.

Had I been that cruel to her that day? I knew I was an asshole - everybody told me so - but I didn't think I'd been that bad. I'd even given her a watch (a reward for mouthing off at me, even if she pretended she hadn't done so).

I slowed down as I neared her, worried I'd startle her if I got too close too quickly. She eventually must have noticed someone coming because she looked up. There was pure sorrow in her eyes. My heart started beating double time, and I felt my fists clench at my side. I wanted to kill whoever had done this to her.

"Who hurt you?" My voice came out rougher than I expected. I took a deep breath and tried again in a softer, calmer voice. "What's wrong, Miss Flynn?"

"It...it's nothing, I'm sorry, I shouldn't be crying here." Her voice was shaky.

"You can cry wherever you fucking please in my building. Just tell me what's wrong so I can fix it."

I may have grown up around violent men, but we respected and cared for the women in our lives. Nobody hurt a woman and got away with it.

"I can't tell you. It's...it's too much. It's not your responsibility to fix anything."

I took her hand in mine. It was soft, delicate, and shaking like a leaf in the wind. She looked up at me with those pretty green eyes the color of sea moss, and I don't know what came over me. In one quick, thoughtless motion, I pulled her into my arms and kissed her.

It was soft and sweet, yet there was some passion behind it. I held my lips firmly against hers, waiting for her to push me away. Instead, she let out a strained sob.

"I'm s-s-sorry."

I let her go but kept my arm around her. She let me hold her as she cried. I felt her body shiver: she must have been freezing. I removed my suit jacket and put it over her shoulders, waiting for her to tell me exactly what was wrong.

It took almost an hour of us sitting there together for her to finally open up. She explained how her father was part of the Irish mob back in Boston, and he'd made a deal with Ronan Sullivan that she'd marry his son.

"Cullen Sullivan?"

"Yes, how do you know who he is?"

"Let's just say, I know a thing or two about the Irish. Not exactly the best of the best when it comes to crime families. The Sullivans are violent and mean, and that's just to their women."

She let out another sob. I knew I'd said the wrong thing.

"You don't have to worry; we'll find a solution. I'm not going to let them get to you, I promise. I'll find a way to fix this."

"How can you be so sure? I mean, I know you're rich and powerful in this world, but that doesn't mean much in theirs. They deal with the seedy side of life - drugs, weapons, extortion."

I didn't know how to explain to my sweet (and sometimes sassy) personal assistant that I wasn't as clean-cut as I looked in my Brioni suit. How do you tell someone who works for you that you're part of one of the most notorious crime families outside of Italy? But if I didn't confess my connections, she wouldn't believe that I could help her. I needed her to believe that she was safe with me. I couldn't explain why I had this urge to protect her, but it came from deep inside. I needed to make sure that she was safe, no matter the cost. I also knew that I could use my father's advice on this one.

"Have you heard of Antonio Romano?"

She looked up at me, wiping at her eyes. It hadn't escaped me on her first day that she was an extremely pretty woman. Even though I was known for being an asshole, I wasn't one of those bastards who hit on their employees.

"Of course, I have. He's the head of the Romano family. Wait..." It seemed to hit her. "Are you a relation? I never put two and two together because I know it's a common Italian surname."

"He's my father. Somehow, I've managed to keep that out of the press with a lot of bribery and good luck. I know you probably don't think much of the Romanos, given your history, but we're not all evil. I mean, we've been known to be on the wrong side of the law, but we have a code of ethics, and one thing we'd never do is bring harm to our women."

She looked up at me with those gorgeous eyes; there was a bit of hope. It was a big responsibility to be among the many who put it there. I knew that I could help her out. I would do whatever it took.

"Do you really think you can fix this?"

"I know I can." I stood up and offered her my hand; hers was still shaking.

At that moment, I desperately wanted to kiss her again, but I knew deep down that it would only lead to trouble. She was in a vulnerable state, and I shouldn't take advantage of her. I was the one who was meant to be helping her, after all.

"Are you heading up to the office now?" Her voice was still wobbly, but I could tell that she was trying her best to keep it steady.

"I was going to, but I think all that can wait until morning. I'll take you home. I don't want you walking around the city in your current state."

"No, you really don't have to do that. I'm fine, really I'm fine. I'm made of far tougher stuff, I swear. This just took me by surprise, that's all."

"I know you're tough stuff, Miss Flynn, but let me get you home. It will put my mind at ease to know you're home safe."

I picked up her purse and swung it over my shoulder, earning a laugh from my assistant. I don't know what had gotten into me the moment I saw her in tears, but it had somehow softened me. Nobody in my life would ever describe me as an overly caring man. In fact, I was known to be a bit of a bastard. I think the word used most often was "cold".

I wasn't a cruel man, not really, not deep down inside. I was just an asshole because that's the type of man who got shit done. I wasn't going to leave a vulnerable woman sitting crying on the steps of my building.

"Good night, Mr. Romano."

"Good night, Clem." I shook hands with the night guard at the front entrance. He was used to me coming and going late at night.

"Do you know everyone in this building by name?" By looking at her, you wouldn't be able to tell that only a few moments ago, my assistant was crying her eyes out. In fact, her eyes looked clearer and shone even more brightly than usual.

"Yep, Dad taught me that. If you want to run an empire - whether that's a company or something a little different - you should know every person's name and, if possible, their story."

"What's Clem's story?"

"He's twice divorced with three kids from his second marriage, who he loves very much. They spend every second weekend with him because he works at night, but he makes sure that when they're with him, they're always doing something fun and meaningful."

"You're not who I thought you were."

"Yes, I am. I'm not a good man, Miss Flynn. Don't take this little act of kindness as a sign that there's more to me. I've done some terrible things, and I don't regret them."

We walked the rest of the way in silence, I dropped her off at her apartment and went back to the office to sort out the new product features. In the morning, I'd figure out what to do about my assistant's situation.

Chapter 3
ARABELLA

♥

Mr. Romano had calmed me down by the time I got home. But I still couldn't sleep. I kept thinking about everything that had happened that night. About Father's phone call and the arrangement for me to marry one of the cruelest men I knew. And...about that strangely intense kiss between my boss and me. In fact, I thought about that kiss more than I should have, given the circumstances. He was just trying to...I don't know, calm me down, maybe? I remembered the taste of his lips, like scotch and a hint of mint. They were strong yet supple and almost soft.

I must have fallen asleep around three am, and my alarm started blaring three hours later. I was exhausted and thought about calling in sick. I didn't think Mr. Romano would mind. But I wasn't going to let him down after everything he'd done the night before. He hadn't needed to be so kind.

I got dressed in a haze, thinking about how I was going to get myself out of this situation. If I stayed in New York, I knew Dad would send one of his men to get me. It wasn't like he hadn't done it to other people. And they likely wouldn't give me a choice. I'd be shoved into the back of a car and taken back to Boston without any say.

I could always go live with my maternal grandmother in Ireland, so I picked up the phone to call her. Even though she lived on an entirely different continent, we'd always been close. When my mother was alive, we'd go visit her every other year; and the years when we didn't, she'd fly to Boston.

She hated my father, but knew that Mother wouldn't leave him. After she died, my grandmother tried to get my sister and me to go and live with her, but Dad wouldn't allow it. He even tried to stop all communication between the two of us. My sister didn't care much, but I did. I'd wait until Father was out drinking with his buddies, and then I'd go to the neighbor and use her phone.

I'd call my grandmother and let it ring three times. She'd call back so my neighbors weren't stuck paying for a long-distance phone call.

I wasn't allowed a cell phone until I turned sixteen; and even then, Father would monitor it closely. I couldn't send a single text without him knowing. It was stifling. By the time I turned twenty-one and had finished my business college, I tried to leave for the first time. I just moved to a different neighborhood, but he'd call me relentlessly and have his men visit me to "make sure I was okay".

Eventually, I ended up moving home. That was when I started saving. At twenty-four years old, I took my savings and moved to New York. I lived off that money until I got the job at Gallbury Tech.

I put down the phone. I didn't even know what time it was in Ireland, although my grandmother always said that she didn't mind what time I called. She was always happy to wake up to talk to me. I could have run away to stay with her, but I had a feeling that Cullen Sullivan wouldn't take the rejection well. I couldn't risk something happening to my grandmother. I would much rather be in danger myself than put that wonderful woman in danger. She was the only family member who ever seemed to really care about me.

My sister said she did. Sometimes we'd get along and even enjoy a good conversation. But she didn't understand why I wanted to stay away from the mob. She'd made it part of her life. She'd married one of Sullivan's men and planned to pop out the next generation of Irish criminals.

I couldn't run away to my grandmother: I couldn't put her in harm's way. All I could do was hope that Mr. Romano would find a way to help me, even though he didn't owe me anything. I was just his assistant, after all. He didn't need to help me.

I didn't like the idea of relying on another man to protect me, but I didn't really have a choice. It was either try whatever he had in mind or get married to Cullen Sullivan, give birth to his children, and live out my life in utter hell. I got dressed in a daze and left my apartment, running into Brian on the staircase. He looked like he was just getting home.

"Hey sweety, what's that frown all about?"

I tried to smile but I came out more of a grimace. "Just a little tired, that's all."

"That's because you work too hard and play too little. Come out tonight, I'll be bartending and can swing you some free drinks. There's going to be a performer, it'll be great."

"I'll think about it."

"I know that means no, but I'll still keep an eye out for you."

And with that, I made my way to the office. I even arrived a little early. I was only supposed to start at 8:30, but I always tried to get there before my boss. That way I could make sure he had some coffee and everything he needed before the day got hectic.

I hadn't beat him to the office that day.

"Miss Flynn, could you come in here, please?" Gone was the softer tone from the night before. His voice was as stern and cold as it usually was.

I was a little nervous as I walked in. Would he be usual asshole self again? Would he go straight back to being cold? Would he give up on helping me and just decide that it wasn't worth his time to help his personal assistant with her personal problems?

"Morning, Mr. Romano, can I get you some coffee?" If he was going to act like the previous night hadn't happened, then I could do the exact same thing.

"No, I'm good for now. Managed to do it all by myself." He picked up his mug to show me he'd already made himself a cup. His voice was dry and sarcastic, nothing like the kindness I'd experienced only hours before.

"What can I do for you?" I had put my professional mask back on and was determined not to remove it again.

"You can close the door. We have something to discuss."

I turned around and closed his door as quietly as possible. I didn't want to alert anyone else to the fact that the two of us were alone together...although, given that I worked for him, it wasn't uncommon. I took a seat opposite him, and he leaned forward on the desk, his shirt sleeves rolled up, exposing his powerful forearms.

"I've spoken to Father and some associates about your issue. There's nothing we can do as the Romano family to interfere in mob matters, especially in Boston. We don't have much power there."

"Well, thank you for trying." I tried to smile, but my stomach was sinking. I knew in that moment that I was well and truly screwed. No one was going to save me. No one could help me. I was going to be traded like cattle to Cullen Sullivan, and there was nothing that I could do about it.

"Hold up. I'm still not giving up. There's nothing we can do officially as the Romano family, but that doesn't mean that there's no hope. There is something you and I can do to ensure that Cullen Sullivan can't get to you."

I felt a flickering of hope.

"And what's that? What can we do? I'll do anything."

"We can get married."

I waited for him to laugh or make any indication that he'd been joking.

"Sorry, what?"

"You and I can get married. If you're married to a Romano, there's no way he'll go after you. He might give your father some shit, but I'm sure you don't care about that. There's no way he's going to come after me or my wife."

"That's a...lot. I mean, that's a lot to ask of you. You don't even know me that well. You have no reason to go to that extent just to help me."

"I can't just sit by and watch you suffer. I'm an asshole, but I'm not that kind of asshole. Anyway, we don't actually have to sign the papers. We just have to put on a show of being married. We can fly to Vegas, get some pictures at the chapel, and let the word spread.

"Your father and the Sullivan family won't be able to do anything about it. And it's not like it's a permanent solution. We just have to pretend to be married until I find another one, and I will find one. I'm a resourceful man, Miss Flynn."

I wasn't too keen on taking the help of another crime family in the first place, let alone considering marrying into one, even if it wasn't technically a real marriage.

"What would we tell people at Gallbury Tech. There's got to be some kind of rule about office dating?"

"I'll call HR this afternoon and set up a meeting letting them know that we intend to get married. Once they're sure you're not going to sue the company for sexual harassment, they won't care too much."

"And you're willing to do this?"

"I don't see what choice I have? I know the Sullivan's reputation, and it's not good. What kind of man would I be if I let you get caught up in all that?"

I wanted to say no. I wanted to say, "Thank you, but I'll figure this out by myself." But I didn't have another option. The Romanos were known for being powerful in the organized crime community and the Sullivans and my father would think more than twice about coming after me if I were married to one of them.

"Okay, so how do we do this? Do we tell people we've been seeing each other for a while? Or do we pretend it's a spur of the moment decision? We have to come up with a story so it doesn't look like it's fake."

"We've been dating for a while now, but we wanted to keep it private. Nobody will argue with that. I've always been a private man. We can fly over to Vegas this weekend. You can move into my apartment when we get back to really sell it and ensure no one questions it."

"And it's just until we figure out another solution?"

"I'll find another way to fix this, I promise. I just need some time, and this will buy us time."

"Okay, let's get fake married." I could hear the words coming out of my mouth, but they didn't even sound like me. I didn't do things like this. I was the type of girl who would plan everything ahead. But this time, I didn't have a choice.

"Great. Go back to your desk. Call up the head of HR and have him meet us in my office in an hour. They won't argue if it's me asking."

I went back to my desk and did exactly as asked. The rest of the day went by in a blur. I went home that evening and started packing my bag for Vegas. I didn't even know what people wore to get married in Vegas. Should I have gotten a wedding dress? I packed a long white maxi dress instead.

Chapter 4

MATTEO

♥

"Have you ever been on a private plane before?" I didn't know why I was asking: I already knew the answer. It's not like most people flew around on personal planes. I was rich, and not stupid.

I had to say something because the woman standing in front of me with a suitcase was absolutely breathtaking. I'd only seen her in her standard work skirt suits. Right then, she was standing in front of me in a long, flowing maroon dress that seemed to fit her form beautifully.

"No, I haven't. Is it much different to flying commercial?"

"It's like the difference between being in a personal car and being on the subway. Are you a nervous flyer?"

"No, I've always been good on flights. I'm used to the trip to Ireland to see my grandmother. The flight to Vegas is a lot shorter I'm guessing." She even laughed a little at that one and the sound made my heart beat a little faster in my chest.

"Well, Miss Flynn, let's get going." I grabbed her bags and walked her onto the plane.

"I think if we're going to be married, or at least pretend to be, we should be on a first name basis."

"Right, that's true, Arabella. And I guess we're going to be telling people it's Mrs. Romano from now on anyway."

She giggled at that; I swear I felt myself getting hard. I took a seat before it became any clearer. She sat down on the couch opposite me and looked around with wonder in her eyes. I couldn't even remember my first time on a private plane as it was so long ago.

· ♥ · ♥ · ♥ · ♥ · ♥ ·

Six hours later, we were in our suite getting ready to pretend to get married. I had some champagne ordered up to the room to keep up the pretense - and also because I thought she might like it. We didn't have to get dressed up, but I thought it might be worth it for the pictures. It had to look like we were really getting married, not doing it for show. If the Sullivans for one second believed that we hadn't actually gotten hitched, they'd be going after her in minutes. I knew their type. They'd treat her even worse because of the lie.

I was wearing one of my Brioni suits, but I opted for a black shirt and no tie. It was Vegas after all. I was getting ready in the bathroom while she got ready in the bedroom. I was going to book a two suites, but I thought that if anyone heard about it, it would lead to trouble down the line. Everything had to look like two lovebirds who'd run away to Vegas to get married in a fit of passion.

I waited an extra ten minutes before knocking on the door to see if she was ready.

"Just a minute."

I stared at myself in the bathroom mirror. Not bad. I knew I cleaned up well. It wasn't like there was ever a shortage of women willing to date me. But I'd never really been interested in them, given that it was complicated with my family. Either women wanted me because I was the billionaire CEO of a tech company or because I was the heir to the Romano throne. I didn't want a relationship that was tied to either of those things.

It was hard for women to see me just for me. But it wasn't like I tried. It's not like I was celibate, I just had affairs rather than relationships - quick, easy, and no mess. Now I was marrying my personal assistant, or at least that's what it would look like to the rest of the world.

"You can come out now."

I had to catch my own breath when I saw her. She was wearing a simple white strappy number that flowed down to her ankles and still managed to hug every curve of her body. Her hair cascaded down her shoulders, and she wore striking red lipstick that made her eyes more prominent.

"You look... phenomenal."

"Right back at you, Mr. Romano." She smiled.

"It's Matteo, remember. We're about to be husband and wife."

· ♥ · ♥ · ♥ · ♥ · ♥ ·

I bribed the chapel to do the ceremony without the paperwork. The woman was as confused as hell, but I think the thick wad of cash I handed over made up for it. We got married by an Elvis impersonator, which wasn't as original as the Johnny Cash impersonator Arabella wanted until we realized that our outfits were almost identical (although mine was obviously more refined).

We got about a hundred pictures of us saying vows, posing with Elvis, and looking like a couple that had just gotten married. When The King announced that we were now husband and wife, I pulled her close and kissed her deeply.

Sure, it was good for the photos, but I'd also wanted to kiss her since I'd seen her in that dress. In fact, I'd wanted to kiss her since I'd kissed her the other night when she cried on the stairwell. There was something about this woman that made me a little crazy. She wasn't like the other women in my life.

"Right, I need a drink, Mrs. Romano." I winked at my fake bride. "Should we grab dinner and a drink?"

"I think that's a wonderful idea, Mr. Romano."

We ate dinner at a five star restaurant where they sent over a bottle of champagne to celebrate the newlyweds. We ate and talked about our favorite movies, books, and music. It was nice for once to just talk about random things and not about business (Gallbury Tech or the Romano family business).

We were a bit tipsy by the time we made it upstairs. As soon as we walked into the room, she kicked off her shoes with a happy sigh and put on some music. It was an old Chuck Berry album, and I laughed as she danced around.

"You have to dance with me! It's our first dance as a married couple!" she announced as Teenage Wedding came on.

It was a teenage wedding and the old folks wished them well..

I laughed and started dancing with her. We were both attempting the twist when she almost tripped over a bag we'd left in the middle of the room. I caught her in my arms and pulled her upright but didn't let her go. Instead, I started swaying with her in my arms.

Before I could stop myself, I was kissing her deeply. I almost pulled away, worried that I'd overstepped, until I heard her softly moan into my lips. I moved my hands to her hips, pulling her flush against me. I could feel myself hardening against her stomach.

In response, she wrapped her arms around neck, pulling me down to get closer to her. If I was waiting for a sign that she was into it as I was, this was it. I grabbed her luscious ass as she ground herself against me. I groaned. I could feel my cock stiffening to the point where it was throbbing.

I kissed her jaw, her neck, moving down until I was unzipping the back of her dress. I shoved the material down until it was pooled at her feet. She was wearing a lacy white bra, and I couldn't help but think that it was meant for me on our "wedding night". Just as I was about to reach around and unclip her bra, she stepped back.

"Your turn, Mr. Romano." There was a glint in her eyes and a wicked smile on her face.

I wasted no time ripping off my shirt (I could afford a new one) and getting rid of my pants. Her eyes widened when my erection sprang free as I lowered my black briefs. I smiled cockily. I was a big guy, and every part of me was in proportion.

That wicked smile of hers only grew as she got on her knees before me. I wasn't going to protest, I liked this forward side of her, but I almost swallowed my tongue as she took me in her tight, wet mouth. She gave me one long, slow suck, and licked the precum off the head. I could barely breathe in that moment. Next thing I knew, she was taking me to the back of her throat, while she softly hummed.

It took everything I had not to come immediately. As much as I wanted her to swallow my cum, I wanted to be inside her more.

When I was on the verge of an orgasm, I stepped back and pulled her up, whipped her around, and bent her over the bed. I pulled down her white silk thong and stuck a thick finger inside her pussy. She was soaking wet. I licked my finger, grabbed my cock and sunk deep inside her.

She gasped as I let her adjust to my size. I waited until her breathing returned to something resembling normal and then I started thrusting. Once we'd built up a rhythm, I pulled her up against my chest and wrapped my hands around her breasts, tweaking her nipples as she loudly moaned.

I waited until I could feel her pussy constricting around me, before lowering my hand to her front and drew circles around her clit. She was screaming my name in no time, and I could feel her orgasm around my cock.

I turned her around and lay her down on the bed; she wrapped her legs around my waist, and I could feel that I was close. I pumped into her until I was sure I was about to burst, pulled out and came on her stomach. Out of breath and exhausted, I fell on the bed next to her, throwing an arm and leg over her and turning her face to kiss me.

We lay like that for a while, just catching our breath in between kisses. Eventually, I got up and found a washcloth, walking over and cleaning her up.

"Sorry about that; we didn't use a condom, and I don't know if you're on birth control."

"It's okay. I'm on birth control, but I prefer to use condoms because sometimes I forget to take them when I'm in a hurry."

・♥・♥・♥・♥・♥・

I woke up with every intention of ordering breakfast in bed for us and starting on round two. But by the time I opened my eyes, Arabella was already out of bed and fully dressed.

"What time is it?"

"It's around seven." She smiled at me, but it wasn't the same smile as the night before.

"Why don't you come back to bed? We have nowhere to be."

"I don't think that's a good idea."

I sighed and sat up, "Didn't you enjoy last night?"

"Oh, I had a great time last night. That was…delightful." There was that giggle again. "I just don't think it should happen again."

"And why exactly is that?"

"It complicates things, and this *arrangement* is already extremely complicated. I don't want us getting confused in the process. I can't afford to have anything go wrong. I appreciate everything you're doing for me, and the lines will get a lot blurrier if we're sleeping together."

She passed me a cup of coffee, and I sat up to drink it. I could feel the disappointment all the way to the pit of my stomach, but I wasn't going to argue with her. Not right then. I knew she was attracted to me, and I was definitely attracted to her. This was going to happen again, but I'd let her believe that it wasn't - if that's what she needed to feel in control.

Chapter 5
ARABELLA

I moved into Matteo's penthouse as soon as we got back from Vegas. He offered to have it done, but I insisted on packing my own things. I didn't want a bunch of strange men rifling through my personal effects. Anyway, I didn't have all that much. Just a few knick knacks, my clothing, and some old photo albums from Mom.

I'd rented the apartment fully furnished. It wasn't the nicest place, but it was all I could afford in the city. Still, it was my first real taste of freedom, and I was going to miss it. I would obviously move into my own place once we'd found a solution to Cullen problem, but I would have to find a new one. I couldn't rent a place I wasn't even living in.

As the men loaded up the moving truck, I went to say goodbye to Brian. It's not like I was leaving the city, but I couldn't just move out and not let him know. He'd been a good friend to me since I'd accidentally tried to get into his apartment.

"Hey, sweetie, what's up?"

I hadn't thought about how I was going to explain this to my only friend, the only person who would've known if I were dating my boss.

"So, I, uh, got married."

"What the actual fuck? Please do come inside and explain yourself."

He poured us each a margarita from the jug he always had in the fridge.

"It was kind of a whirlwind romance kind of thing. We just got back from Vegas."

"I'm shocked…you went to Vegas without me? I'll forgive you just this once. But do it again and we're over. I'm serious, Bella. How did you meet this handsome stranger? I assume he's handsome if he got you to marry him in Vegas."

"Well, he's technically my boss."

"Technically?"

"I mean, he is 100% my boss…the CEO of Gallbury Tech."

"Oh, holy shit. It's always the ones you don't think it'll be. At least tell me there was no time for a prenup?"

I giggled and took a sip of margarita. "It's not like that."

There was a knock at the door. I knew it would be the guys with the truck wanting to get a move on. I downed the last of my drink and kissed Brian on the cheek.

"I promise to come by the bar and tell you more. But right now, I have to get going. My new husband will be wondering where I am."

"You're full of surprises, Bella, full of surprises."

· ♥ · ♥ · ♥ · ♥ · ♥ ·

I spent the rest of the afternoon unpacking my things in Matteo's guest bedroom. I don't know why I thought we'd be sharing a room, especially after I told him that we couldn't sleep together again. It just seemed weird to be living as "husband and wife" and have my own room and bathroom.

His penthouse apartment was spacious, to say the least. I don't know what else I expected of the billionaire tech CEO (and son of the head of the Romano crime family). It was also a really warm and inviting space. I could tell he enjoyed his time here. It wasn't cold and clinical like I'd always imagined his home would be. Then again, I'd come to realize that the man he was at work wasn't necessarily the man he was off the clock.

When I eventually left my room to get a glass of water, I found my new "husband" in the kitchen, sipping coffee. He was barefoot in a pair of well-worn, yet perfectly fitted, jeans and a Henley. I'd never seen him looking so relaxed. It took everything I had not to walk up behind him and wrap my arms around him.

"All settled in?"

"Yep, the room is lovely. I think it's bigger than my whole apartment."

"Don't just think you have to stay in there. The whole place is yours as long as you stay here. I want you to feel at home."

"Thank you, I really appreciate you doing all this for me."

"Talking about home...I thought it'd be nice for you to come to family dinner tonight. As far as anyone aside from us knows, you're my wife. I think my mother and sisters would cut my head off if I didn't bring you to dinner. They're already pissed about the Vegas wedding."

I paused for a minute. I hadn't thought about the fact that I would essentially be a Romano woman for as long as we pretended to be married. I wasn't exactly dying to get involved with another crime family. But if the Romano men were all like Matteo, I didn't feel so bad about it. After all, it was only until we came up with another solution.

"Well, you have a nice head, so it would be a shame to have it cut off." I smiled at him.

"Oh, honey, you have no idea how nice my *head* is." With that he got up, put his cup in the dishwasher, and walked away, leaving me stunned.

I didn't know how much of his flirting I could take without giving in. Maybe that was something we should have talked about. But I decided that I could wait until after dinner with his family.

· ♥ · ♥ · ♥ · ♥ · ♥ ·

"You must be Arabella! We're so excited to meet the one woman able to capture Matteo's attention." A woman in her sixties with a sleek gray bob pulled me into a hug the second I walked into the Romano family home.

It wasn't really a house; it was far more like a mansion out of a fairytale. It had a gorgeous wraparound porch, something out of place on the Upper East Side. But it somehow looked perfect in its surroundings.

"Here are Zita, Mara, and Louise. Zita and Mara are mine, and Mara is married to my other son Luciano."

"I can't believe my big brother actually got married. We didn't think it would ever happen. You must be one magical lady." Zita kissed me on the cheek while Mara gave me a quick once over.

"Couldn't have waited to have a proper wedding?" I could tell that it would take a little more than walking in through the front door to win Mara over.

"It was a spur of the moment kind of thing. I meant no offense to the family, I promise."

"Mara, it was all my doing. You want to give someone grief, give it to me, not my wife. The poor woman is meeting you crazy women for the first time. Try to play nice." Matteo wrapped his arm around me and kissed me on the cheek.

It was all for show, but it still felt nice. I'd never really had a proper boyfriend, not a proper one, anyway. Any time a guy had shown any interest in me, Dad or my brother-in-law would send him a message. The only boys I was allowed to date were connected to the mob, and I wanted nothing to do with them.

Funny how things work out.

"Okay, okay, I promise I'm nicer than I came across at first. I just take some time to warm up. That's what happens when you grow up with brothers like Matteo and Luciano."

I smiled at Mara. Both her and her sister were exceptionally striking with their dark hair, big eyes, and olive skin. "Well then, I'll have to try my best to win you over."

"Arabella?" an older male voice came from behind me. I turned around to face an older version of Matteo. Even though the man's hair was gray and the years had clearly taken their toll on his skin, he was clearly Antonio Romano, Matteo's father and the head of the Romano crime family.

"Yes, sir." My palms started sweating. He was the one person who knew the truth about Matteo and my marriage.

"Welcome to the family." His smile was big and genuine as he bent down to kiss me on the cheek. "You must be something special to win over my Matteo."

There must have been around twelve people at dinner: the four siblings, their spouses, Matteo's parents, and two cousins. The children were apparently being babysat so the grownups could have a bit of peace and quiet - although there was nothing quiet about this big family dinner.

Everyone was super nice; even Mara warmed up to me by the time she'd had a glass or two of red wine. It felt like a real family, something I had never really experienced growing up. It was big and loud and filled with love. I couldn't imagine Antonio threatening his daughters. I couldn't even imagine him grounding them growing up.

"So, Arabella, what's your family like?" Adrienne, Matteo's mother, refilled my wine glass.

"Nothing like this, I can promise you. It was just Dad and my sister after Mom passed away. Very quiet upbringing."

"I'm really sorry to hear about your mother. A girl needs a mother."

"I always had my grandmother, but she lives in Ireland. I haven't seen her in a few years, but I'm planning to take a trip there at the end of the year. I'm just saving up."

"You've married a billionaire, I don't think you need to worry about saving up any more."

"Luciano, that was rude. Apologize to my wife, before I smack you upside the head."

"Sorry, Arabella, I wasn't trying to be rude. Just stating a fact. Matteo could fire up the jet and have you in Ireland next week if you wanted. What I meant is that you don't have to worry about money when you're a Romano. We take care of our own."

I just took a sip of my wine, feeling weird about the whole money thing. Matteo and I hadn't discussed money at all. I mean, I knew that he was a billionaire, but we weren't even really married, so I wasn't entitled to anything from him.

It was enough that I got to live rent-free in his apartment, which would help me save for a while. Until we found another solution, anyway. Then I would go my way, and he would go his. The rest of the evening went along nicely. Everyone was so warm, and it was clear that this was a loving and caring family.

After dinner, I helped the women clear up in the kitchen while Matteo, Luciano, and Antonio had a talk on the porch. It was nice; there was music playing while we stacked the dishwasher and put away the leftovers.

After a while, Matteo came over and wrapped his arms around me from behind. "Let's get home, wife."

"Ah, the joy of being newlyweds." Zita raised her glass at us. "Are you at least taking your new wife on a honeymoon?"

Matteo looked at me and I raised my eyebrows, unsure of what to say. He eventually answered for both of us. "Things are a bit hectic at work at the moment. We'll definitely plan a trip in a few months. We just can't take the time away at the moment."

"Always with the work. Just like your father." Adrienne lovingly patted her son on the cheek.

The drive home wasn't too long and we sat in an easy silence.

"Your family are amazing." I kicked my shoes off as soon as we got into the apartment. Matteo did the same, both of us leaving our shoes at the door.

"We can be a bit loud and obnoxious, but they're good people."

"You're a good person too, you know."

"Trust me, Arabella, I'm not a good guy. I won't hurt you. I wouldn't do that. But I've done my fair share of bad things."

Chapter 6

MATTEO

♥

I had a good time with my family and Arabella. I could honestly say I had a great time. She really fit in with my sisters, their husbands, and my parents. I felt a little guilty about how excited Mother was about us getting married. For security reasons, my father was the only one who knew that this marriage was fake.

It wasn't that I couldn't trust the rest of my family, I just didn't want to get them involved. There was a blanket rule in the Romano family, you didn't get anyone involved in shady shit unless you absolutely had to, especially when it came to the women.

I stretched out on my bed and thought about what I'd gotten myself into. I wasn't worried about the Irish mob. They weren't great people, known for their senseless violence and drinking, but they weren't an outright threat to us. They weren't stupid enough to attack us on our territory, even though I'd essentially insulted them by marrying a woman who was promised to the son of their leader.

Overall, being married to Arabella wasn't the worst thing to happen to me. Honestly, I couldn't stop replaying our wedding night over and over again in my mind. I instantly got hard as I thought about her naked body and how wet she was for me. I readjusted my erection in my sweatpants.

I knew that I couldn't fall for her. Arabella was a good woman. She didn't want to be involved in another crime syndicate, and I wasn't likely going to leave my whole family behind at any point. Even though she'd seemed to enjoy herself at dinner, she was hesitant because of what my family did to earn our money.

It wasn't like I really wanted a wife. I worked long hours, trying to keep my family responsibilities separate from my work at Gallbury Tech. I'd always promised myself that I'd stay single for as long as I was involved in my father's business, and if I took over as head of the family business, I'd never settle down.

I'd never really been the commitment type, anyway. The longest relationship I'd had until that point had been three months, and that was mostly because I hadn't found the time to break up with her. It just seemed easier to continue going on dates until she started asking questions about the future.

I was tossing and turning that night, feeling all kinds of uncomfortable with the situation I'd put myself in. I got up to go and get myself a drink, and maybe watch something on TV. When I got to the kitchen, Arabella was sitting there drinking herbal tea.

"Can't sleep either?" Her voice was so soft and sweet that it actually irritated me. How could she be so comfortable with this whole situation? Didn't she hate people like me? People who broke the law and took what they wanted?

I just grunted my response and pulled a bottle of scotch from the cupboard. I knew it didn't make sense for me to be angry with her; and to be completely honest, I wasn't. I was upset with myself for a whole range of reasons...mostly because I didn't actually know what the hell I was going to do with this woman.

"Wow, you're awfully talkative tonight." She flashed me a sarcastic smile.

"I'm just trying to pour myself a drink. Can I do that without some kind of running commentary?"

I knew I was acting like an asshole. I was well aware that my behavior was unacceptable, but I didn't really give a fuck at that moment. I was tired and in a bad mood. Usually there was no one around to witness me at my worst, although I hadn't exactly been warm and fuzzy to my assistant, leading up to when I suggested we get married.

"How do you go from being the sweet and lovely man you were at dinner to a completely cold asshole a few hours later?" I'd obviously struck a nerve, and my pretend wife wasn't going to stand for it.

"You know this whole marriage thing is fake, right? You don't actually have to be a nagging wife when it's just the two of us at home alone."

I was well aware that I'd crossed some kind of line, and it would be hard to come back from it. I was about to apologize when she turned around and slammed her empty tea cup on the table so hard that a crack spread up the side of it.

"Fuck you, Matteo. One minute you're wanting to play like you're my savior and the next, you're being a complete dickhead. Which one are you?"

"I'm a complex human being, Miss Flynn." I threw back my scotch and poured another.

She actually laughed at that. "No, you're just a man who's always gotten what he wants and never had to think twice about the way he behaves."

And with that, she marched away...or at least tried to.

I whipped my arm out, grabbing her around the waist and pulling her to me. Her shock was clear on her face, but it kept her quiet as I pressed my lips to hers, demanding entrance. She hesitated at first, keeping her mouth firmly shut, but as I glided my tongue against her bottom lip, she seemed to melt into my iron grip.

I kissed her furiously, angrily and passionately. Every emotion that I was trying to escape went into that kiss. I knew that she wanted me as much as I wanted her, she just didn't want to want me. But it didn't take much to get her to give in to her desires.

I pushed her up against the kitchen door, continuing to grasp her around the waist. I ground my erection into her core and nearly came as she moaned into my mouth. I pulled on the lacy string that tied around her, opening her robe and leaving me with a full view of her in matching white lingerie. I took a slight step back to admire the view and audibly groaned.

Arabella's cheeks reddened as I stared at her, slowly stroking myself through my sweatpants. Just as I thought she was going to shy away from the whole situation, she moved her right hand down her bare stomach and slid them into her white lacy panties. I didn't think there was a sexier sight in the whole world.

Her mouth opened with a gasp as she slowly began to pleasure herself. I sunk to my knees in front of her, slowly pulling down her underwear to reveal her glistening pussy. I took her hand in mine and pulled her fingers to my lips, sucking all the wetness from them, basking in the taste of her.

"Fuck me, you taste like heaven. I need more." And with that, I spread her lips, running my tongue down her center to her core, fully tasting her.

My favorite part was how she reacted to me, like I was a long lost lover she couldn't wait to touch again. She nearly came apart as I sucked her clit into my mouth. I gave it a lengthy pull as she cried out my name. As I circled her clit with the tip of my tongue, I used two fingers to slowly to fuck her tight pussy. She cried out as I increased the speed and licked harder and more intensely. I could feel the precum leaking into my briefs. I needed to be inside her as soon as possible.

First, I needed her to come. I increased the speed at which I was fingering her and sucked her clit into my mouth as her pussy started clamping down on me. She put her hands on my shoulders, shifting her weight to me as her legs started shaking uncontrollably.

As she came down from her high, I picked her up as I stood to my full height. She giggled as I threw her over my shoulder fireman-style and carried her to the couch in the living room. It was the second sweetest thing I'd ever heard, the first was her screaming my name. I whipped off my shirt and stepped out of my sweatpants and briefs. I was already rock hard and ready for her. I stroked myself from base to tip really slowly as she watched.

"You want me inside you? You want me to fuck you?"

"Yes," her voice was breathy with anticipation.

"I need you to ask nicely."

"Please fuck me, Matteo. Are you going to make me beg you."

"Not tonight." I winked at her.

I sat down next to her and she looked at me a little confused.

"What are you doing?" She raised an eyebrow skeptically.

"I want you to ride me, baby. I want you to take my cock the way you want it."

She didn't even hesitate. She swung a leg over me, spread her thighs and positioned her core.

Even though we'd had sex recently, I wasn't prepared for how good she felt as she sank down on me. I thought I was going to come too soon as she started moving up and down on my shaft, her mouth open with soft gasps. At first, she took me slowly, but as her orgasm began to build, she started moving faster and faster until I grabbed her ass and decided to help her out. We moved together like we'd choreographed our movements.

"We're so good together." My voice was rough with lust.

"Yes, we are." Her voice was barely audible, but I knew exactly what she was saying.

Her pussy convulsed with her second orgasm of the night. I let her ride it out and then flipped us around so I was on top. It was like I'd been possessed, and the only thing in the world that mattered was the two of us.

I remembered just in time that I wasn't wearing a condom (again) and pulled out to come on her tits as she lay there, breathing heavily with a blissed out look on her face. She'd said she was on the pill, but wasn't great at remembering to take it.

"Baby, if we're going to end up fucking like this, you're going to need to get better at taking the pill, or I'm going to need to remember to wear a condom."

"Who said it would happen again?" She was smiling and there was an evil twinkle in her eye.

"You telling me that wasn't the best fucking orgasm you've ever had?"

"Pretty confident, aren't you?"

She was about to get up, but I stopped her. I picked up my shirt off the floor and cleaned off her perfect tits. Then I kissed her deeply, picking her and carrying her to my bedroom. It didn't seem right to sleep alone after the way we'd just fucked. I promised myself that I wouldn't get attached, but that didn't mean that I couldn't have fun. After we woke up in the morning, I would distance myself from her. I'd tell her that we couldn't be together. But right at that moment, I didn't like the argument I was making to myself.

It would only end in disaster if I tried to form a relationship with her. The whole situation was complicated as it was, and I didn't need to complicate it further. No matter how good we could make each other feel, that didn't mean there was something more to it. Anything more would leave us both feeling like shit...with the best possible outcome. The worst possible outcome?

I end up breaking her heart and fucking up my own life in the process. I decided that in the morning, we'd have to talk. But that night, I slept better than I had in years.

Chapter 7

ARABELLA

♥

When I woke up, Matteo was already up and dressed. As much as I wanted to stay in, I felt awkward lying in his bed without him. I got up and went to join him in the kitchen. As soon as I walked in, I had vivid flashbacks to the night before. I could feel my face going blood red.

"Good morning."

"Morning," he all but grunted.

"Did you sleep well?" Even if he'd been tossing and turning all night, it felt like the only thing to say to him.

He was being surprisingly cold this morning, and I hated it. I felt like a dirty one-night stand that he was trying to get out of his apartment, even though I lived there. I couldn't even get away from him to go to work because first, he was my boss and second, we both had the week off to settle into our marriage supposedly.

The HR director had suggested it. We'd agreed because it made our relationship look legitimate, but the only reason it had been put forward was because they wanted to give the rest of the company time to come to terms with the fact that the CEO had married his personal assistant.

Matteo ignored my awkward question and pushed out the seat opposite him with his foot. "Take a seat, I think we need to talk."

"Can I get some coffee first?" I didn't like the cold tone in his voice. This wasn't my fault. We'd both given in to temptation the night before.

"Sure." He barely even looked at me as I poured myself a cup of coffee from the still-hot pot.

"Right, so what do you want to talk about." I took a sip and scalded my mouth, but swallowed so I wouldn't look like an idiot.

"I don't want you to get the wrong impression after last night. This thing between us isn't real. It can't be real. We're putting on a show so that the Sullivan asshole doesn't think he has a right to the rest of your life. But I don't want you getting any ideas of this actually turning into something. We'll put on a good show for my family, your family, and the office. The rest of the time, we both need to remember that this is only a temporary fix."

After that little speech, my face was red for a whole other reason. How dare that fucker! We were both responsible for what happened the night before. It wasn't like I'd come onto him. In fact, I was the one who originally said we shouldn't let ourselves get confused. I wanted to punch him in the face. I also needed to live with the asshole, so I just sat there for a moment.

"No problem. I really wasn't getting any ideas, Matteo. Believe me, I know I'm just a problem you're trying to solve."

With that, I got up and made my way to my bedroom. He said something as I left, but I was too enraged to actually hear it. I made sure not to slam my door; I didn't want him to think I was upset because he didn't want me. I didn't want him! I didn't want anyone. All I wanted when I moved to New York was to be by myself. I didn't care that I had no friends or support in the city. I'd just wanted to get away from Dad and his mobster friends in Boston. I wanted peace and tranquility...and all I ended up doing was getting fake married to an even bigger criminal.

I took a super-long shower, not caring how much hot water I was using. Growing up, I always had to make sure to save some hot water for the rest of my family. But I didn't care if Matteo didn't have hot water for the rest of his miserable life. Of course, I didn't think a penthouse apartment that belonged to a billionaire would run out of hot water.

I got dressed with the intention to meet up with Brian and have a few margaritas. He'd probably still be sleeping, but he wouldn't mind me waking him up if there was booze involved. Just as I put the last finishing touches on my makeup, Matteo knocked on my door.

"Can I help you?"

"The doorman just rang up, there's someone downstairs claiming to be your sister."

"Oh shit. Oh no. Not Riana. She can't be here. She'll tell my father everything!"

"We'll just have to put on a show for her; it's not that bad. Relax. My family believed us yesterday, and she'll believe us today. It's not that hard."

"Did you let her up?"

"I thought we'd go down and tell her we were on our way to breakfast and invite her with us. That way, we're not stuck in the apartment where she can scrutinize everything."

We made our way down to the impressive lobby. My sister was at the front desk, insisting she be let up to her sister's apartment. As per usual, she was loud and obnoxious. I forced a fake smile on my face and went over to her.

"Riana, what a pleasant surprise!"

"Well, my baby sister got married, and I had to hear it from Dad. I had to come to meet the man who stole your heart."

What she really meant was that she had to check if it was legit and report back to Father like the obedient mob wife and daughter she was.

"Hi, I'm Matteo. It's a pleasure to meet you." Matteo shook her hand with a little too much vigor. I swear I saw her hide a wince. "We were on our way out to breakfast, would you like to join us?"

"Yeah, I suppose I could."

"How long are you here for? Should have let us know so we could have set up the guest bedroom." Matteo was smooth, that was for sure.

"Oh no, Mikey and I are staying at his cousin's place in Queens and going back tomorrow afternoon. Thanks for the offer, though."

I knew that there was no way that Mikey, deep in the Irish mob, would be stupid enough to be caught staying with a Romano, even if that Romano was supposedly his brother-in-law. By the time we got outside, Matteo's driver was ready and waiting. I could tell that my sister was impressed, even though she really didn't want to be. I assumed we'd go to some fancy five-star restaurant so that my new "husband" could show off. But I was surprised when we stopped outside a small coffee shop that looked like it was owned by someone's grandparents.

"A little bit of a weird choice for a billionaire," my sister whispered in my ear as we walked inside.

"He's not a show-off like the men in Boston." I couldn't believe I was defending Matteo after what he'd said that morning, but I was being honest.

"Matteo! Always so good to see you." The old woman behind the counter beamed at my husband.

"Well, I had to introduce you to my new wife," he smiled back. "I had to introduce her to your chocolate chip pancakes and blueberry muffins."

I couldn't help it; I loved the idea of it. I was starving as I hadn't eaten anything since dinner the night before. I hadn't wanted to go to the kitchen after my little talk with Matteo.

"Your wife? This is lovely news! I always said you were too handsome to be on your own. I'll put together a nice little platter for the three of you so your bride can sample all our goods."

He wasn't lying. The choc chip pancakes were probably the best I'd ever tasted, and I'd tried my fair share. I wasn't usually a blueberry muffin girl, preferring cappuccino or classic chocolate, but the mini blueberry muffins she dropped off were to die for. I probably ate one or two too many.

The little old lady introduced herself to me as Matilda. Apparently, Matteo had been coming to the coffee shop since he was an awkward teenager bringing his dates there. I laughed as Matilda told us all about how Matteo would try to romance the girls with flowers and sweet treats.

"He was a spotty little thing back then, but he always had a charming side the girls couldn't resist."

"I think they resisted me perfectly fine back then."

"You did grow into your looks, love."

I couldn't imagine Matteo as anything other than the strong, striking, frankly gorgeous man that he was. He may have been an asshole, but he was damn good-looking. Even my sister couldn't lie and say that he wasn't blisteringly hot.

After breakfast, we took a drive to an art gallery in Brooklyn. My sister wasn't exactly over-the-moon about going to look at art. Her idea of "art" was the old paintings of dogs playing poker that were so popular during the 90s. But she wasn't going to out herself as being uncultured in front of her new billionaire brother-in-law.

After all, she was there to check up on whether our marriage was real, not have a nice day in the city. I really wished that my dad hadn't sent her. It's not that I didn't love my sister, I did. But we'd never been close. She'd always been daddy's girl, whereas I'd been the wayward child that, well, let's just say that my father and I hadn't seen eye-to-eye on a lot of issues.

I, on the other hand, loved the art gallery. the small boutique-style place housed some modern artworks, including a small marble statue of a hand holding a bowl of rings that I couldn't stop staring at. I don't know why it captivated me so much, but it made think of Mom.

It was like the dainty hand was showing the world all of a woman's emotions and thoughts. It was vulnerable and beautiful while still being strong and striking. It made me think of my mother. I could almost feel myself soften while looking at it.

We met the artist Rose Tarning, apparently an old friend of Matteo's sister Mara. She was stunningly beautiful in an almost haunted way; and for a split second, I felt a pang of jealousy when Matteo wrapped her in a hug. But then he stepped back, put his arm around me, and pulled me in for a chaste kiss. If I'd been an audience member, I would have believed that we were happy newlyweds.

Later that afternoon, we took a walk around Central Park with my sister going on and on about how great her husband was doing. I'd known Mikey since I was a kid. He was a dimwitted shithead, but I wasn't going to tell my sister the truth. It wasn't that she'd ever been head over heels in love with him. But Father had introduced them as teenagers, and that was that. With Riana, what Dad says always goes, and he wanted Mikey in the family. I could tell my sister really wanted Matteo to think they were doing great.

It wasn't like we'd grown up poor, as we were solid middle-class. But when you're middle-class and part of a criminal organization, it means you're not a very good criminal. We probably would have been more well off if Father hadn't drunk away every cent he had earned. We mostly lived off Mom's life insurance policy.

We dropped my sister off in Queens so she could have dinner with Mikey and his cousin's family. Matteo had invited both of them to dinner at an upmarket restaurant in Manhattan, but my sister explained that it was the only time she had to see the family.

What she really meant was that Mikey couldn't be seen out and about with Romano.

Chapter 8
MATTEO

While I couldn't say that I was a fan of Arabella's sister, our day together had actually been quite pleasant. I took them to my favorite little coffee shop because I wanted to show Riana that I was introducing my new wife to the people in my life that mattered. Of course, I wasn't going to take it as far as to bring her to my family...that would have been a disaster.

We - the Romano family - had never had any particular issue with the Sullivans and the Irish mob, but we were not even close to being friendly. We were adversaries who didn't bother with each other. They stayed out of New York, and we stayed out of Boston; that's the way it had always worked.

"Thank you for putting up with my sister. I know dealing with my family wasn't part of the plan."

We'd just gotten home after dropping Riana off at her husband's cousin's place. I was glad that she wasn't staying with us. I was scared for a moment that she was going to accept my offer. But I knew that her husband was working for the Sullivans and staying at my place would most certainly cause issues. Still, if she'd said yes to test us, it would have been a problem. It was very clear when you walked into the apartment that it was my place and Arabella was just a guest staying in one of the spare bedrooms.

"No problem. When I agreed to this whole situation, I had a feeling I'd have to prove that we were actually together to the Flynn family. I'm just glad that it wasn't your father. I don't know if I could have remained pleasant with him after what he did to you."

"Well, you were wonderful to my sister. I don't think that there is a single doubt in her head about us. We really pulled off being in a loving relationship."

I didn't like the coldness in her voice; she sounded detached from the whole situation. I'd been the one to start with it that morning, but I just didn't want either of us getting confused about what we were. We didn't have a future - no matter how much chemistry there was between us - and we both knew that.

"Yeah, I think we did good. You hungry? I'm starving. Want to order in some Chinese takeout? I know this great little place that does the best dim sum."

She hesitated for a moment and then nodded her head. "I could eat a horse. It feels like days since we had breakfast. Although, I have to give it to you straight, those were the best pancakes I've ever had, and I will be going back there."

"I told you, didn't I? Best pancakes in New York City. It's family owned as well, which is really nice. It seems like everywhere you look, there's a Starbucks taking over a place that used to be a mom and pop shop. I prefer places with a little bit of soul."

"Me too."

· ♥ · ♥ · ♥ · ♥ · ♥ ·

We ate dinner in front of the big screen TV in the living room. We watched some Romcom from the 90s. I didn't really pay much attention to the screen. Every time Arabella laughed or cringed, my thoughts were consumed with her.

She really was a beautiful woman, and I had to remind myself that I couldn't afford to get attached. Even if I could, she didn't want to get involved with another crime family. I may not have been the head of the Romano family, but it was in my future. There were expectations when it came to me and my responsibility to my family. It wasn't necessarily what I wanted, but that didn't change the reality of it all.

As much as I wanted to curl up with my fake wife on the couch and feel the warmth of her in my arms, I knew that it would only lead to trouble. I'd hated giving her that speech that morning, but it had been for both of our benefit.

After the movie, we said goodnight and went to our respective bedrooms. Her scent was still lingering in my sheets, and I could feel myself getting hard as I breathed her in. I got up and took a cold shower to make sure that I didn't do anything stupid.

That night, I tossed and turned, getting very little sleep.

・♥・♥・♥・♥・♥・

The next morning, I woke up to a text from my father.

Matteo, we need to talk. Something's happened. I'll be at the restaurant at 8 am.

I got up, took another shower and put the coffee on for Arabella before leaving. I made sure to leave a note telling her that I'd gone to see my family. I didn't want her to wake up to an empty apartment and not know where I was. We may not have been in a real relationship, but we were living together until I could sort out the situation.

I ignored the "closed" sign on the door of the old Italian restaurant and made my way to the back room where Father, two of his men, and my brother were sitting deep in conversation.

"Matteo, so glad you could make it." Father had a stiff smile on his face, letting me know that something was definitely wrong.

"Given you're the reason we're all here, I should hope you could fucking make it." My brother clearly wasn't in a great mood.

"The reason we're all here?" I was confused. Why would everyone be meeting because of me? I hadn't even spoken to my family since the dinner at my parent's place. I certainly hadn't been involved in any family business.

"The fucking Sullivans and their dogs had ransacked one of our warehouses just outside the city. Went in with guns blazing and cleared us out. Killed four of our men and left three knocked out. Took the whole stash - weapons and all. They didn't even try to hide who they were. This was clearly a message."

"Message for me?" I knew the answer already. "They're pissed about my marriage and are taking it out on the family."

"We haven't had any difficulty with the Sullivans since the 90s. We'll have to send a message back: tell those inbreds that we' are not to be fucked with."

I hadn't thought that the Sullivans would be stupid enough to retaliate after I had married Arabella. I assumed they'd be pissed off about it, but I thought they'd just fucking drink too much and start a fight with their own people. I didn't think they'd be stupid enough to come after us.

"What's the plan?"

"That's what we're here to figure out, asshole." Wow, my brother was certainly in a fucking mood. I get that this was all because of Arabella. He didn't know that I was trying to save her, but if all that had been caused by our marriage, we'd have been on his side.

We spent the rest of the day making plans to cut off the Sullivan family's supply of weapons and take over two of their warehouses in Boston. We'd managed to pay off enough of their guys to have full access to them. They liked to play like they were in the big leagues, but they were no competition for us. It was all ego on their end, and pride always comes before a fall.

After we'd made solid plans, we made house visits to the widows of the men who'd been killed the night before. We ensured they were taken care of financially and even though we knew that it wouldn't help in the moment, it would at least give them some peace of mind going forward.

We followed that with a visit to our men still in the hospital. We also paid off the nurses and doctors to ensure that nothing got back to the police. It was common business to have connections at the local hospitals near our warehouses in case anything went down.

At the end of the day, I was exhausted. My brother had been as absolute fucking asshole the entire time, even though Father had tried to put him in his place multiple times. Nobody wanted this to happen, and it wasn't like any of us thought they would retaliate. We didn't even think they could get their shit together long enough to plan anything like that.

By the time I got home, all I wanted was a drink and my bed. But as soon as I walked in the apartment, there was music playing and conversation happening in the living room. It's not like I'd told Arabella she couldn't have people over. It was her place as much as mine as long as she was staying with me.

Something in me snapped. She was dancing with a margarita in her hand with some tall guy who looked like a model. In my living room. In my house. While she was supposed to be married to me - according to the outside world, at least. It felt disrespectful.

"What the fuck is going on here?" Even I was slightly shocked by the harsh tone of my voice. I wasn't in the mood to apologize or even think twice about what I was doing.

"Hey Matteo, this is my friend, Brian." Arabella was all giggly and glassy-eyed; she'd clearly had a drink or two already.

The male model walked toward me with his hand out. I ignored it.

"I don't give a fuck who this guy is. I want him out of my apartment. Now."

"So, I'm not allowed to have friends over?" All the joy had left the room.

I didn't bother replying, just went to shut off my record player.

"I'm just going to leave. You be good, my love." The male model said as he gave her a quick kiss on the cheek. I wanted to punch him in the face. It took all I had to keep my hands to myself.

I stayed put as Arabella walked her friend to the door, waiting for her to return so she could explain herself.

"What is wrong with you?! You were out all day. Did you expect me to just stay home and do nothing? Am I not allowed to have friends?"

"You're allowed to have friends. But that man didn't exactly look like a friend. He looked like he wanted to rip your clothes off and fuck you on my sofa."

All the color drained out of my fake wife's face.

"You're an asshole, you know that? Brian's just a friend. Unlike you, he actually wants to spend time with me. And for your information, he's not interested in women!"

I walked over to where she was standing and made a swift movement to grab the bottle of scotch on the bar cart behind her. I hadn't meant to move so quickly, but I wasn't prepared for her reaction. Arabella flinched hard and pulled her arms up to cover her head. She clearly thought I was going to hit her. It was obviously a reflex. Someone in her life had abused her enough that her first reaction when a man got close in anger was to shield herself. I instantly paled.

"Are you okay?" I kept my voice soft so as not to startle her further.

She didn't say anything, but the tears streaming down her face said it all. I watched as she fled the room and ran to her bedroom. I had to stop myself from going after her. I needed to calm down; then I could go and talk to her properly. I didn't want to scare her any more than I already had.

Chapter 9

ARABELLA

I was shaking as I sat on my bed. I looked over at the full-length mirror mounted on the wall and saw that I was as pale as a sheet of paper. I was almost ghostly in appearance with tears streaming down my face. I would have been embarrassed, but I was too freaked out.

I knew Matteo wouldn't hurt me; he wasn't that type of guy. But at that moment when he came toward me with a grim look on his face, it reminded me of the many dark situations I'd been in before in my life.

I could hear Matteo pacing in the hallway outside my bedroom door. The last thing I wanted was for him to come in and see me like that. I was relieved when I heard him walk down the hall to his bedroom and close the door behind him. I was going to have to talk to him about it at some point, but I wasn't ready just yet.

I took a hot shower and put some music on to help clear my head, but I couldn't shake the intense feeling of vulnerability. I also felt incredibly guilty for the way I had responded to Matteo. He was being an asshole, that's for sure, but I had no reason to ever believe that he would lay a hand on me in anger.

After I dried off, I put on a simple silk nightgown and got into bed. Even though I was exhausted, I couldn't calm down enough to get some sleep. I hadn't eaten dinner as Brian and I had planned to order pizzas before Matteo came home and threw his little tantrum.

I made my way through to the kitchen and put together a simple sandwich. I considered making Matteo one, but when I thought about the way he'd lost his temper earlier, I didn't feel like he deserved my kindness. I ate in silence and returned to my room. I'd been tossing and turning for about an hour when there came a soft knock on my door. I looked at the alarm clock on the bedside table next to my bed and saw that it was nearly midnight.

"You can come in."

Matteo walked in slowly. He was wearing a pair of soft gray sweatpants and a simple white tee. Even dressed down with his hair all tousled like he'd been in bed, he looked so damn gorgeous. Honestly, I didn't think there was a single outfit he could be in that would make him unattractive. It almost made me hate him.

"Arabella, I am so fucking sorry." His voice was soft and he sounded tormented, like he'd been replaying the scene in his head over and over again.

"You can't speak to me like that. I don't care what I've done, but you don't get to talk to me like I'm your enemy. Brian is just a friend, and the whole thing was completely innocent. You left for the day and came back in a bad mood, wanting to take it out on me. That's unacceptable. I don't care that you're helping me out and doing me a huge favor; you don't get to treat me like that."

"You're entirely right. I never should have said those things. I want you to feel comfortable enough to have your friends over. As long as we're in this fake marriage, I want you to treat this space as if it is your own. This is your home as much as it is mine. I shouldn't have reacted that way."

"Then why did you?"

For a moment, it didn't look like he was going to reply to me. But then he sat down on the corner of my bed and sighed.

"I had a really difficult day. I know that's no excuse. I was tired and stressed, and I took it out on you and for that I'm truly sorry."

"What happened?"

"Honestly, do you want to know? It's a family business."

I thought about it for a minute. I didn't really want to be involved too much with the Romanos. I'd spent my life around criminals and knew that the more you asked questions, the more involved you became.

"No, as long as I know that you're safe and okay, I don't want to know. Don't take that to mean I don't care, I do, it's just...it's complicated when it comes to the life you live. I can't let myself get in too deep."

"I understand." He leaned forward and softly picked up my foot, putting it in his lap and rubbing the sole in soft little circles.

"It feels like there's something else you want to talk to me about?" I almost didn't ask because I had a feeling about what had him sticking around.

"There is. I have to know, Arabella, why did you flinch when I reached for the bottle of scotch? Did someone hurt you?"

I'd never told anyone before. There'd been one teacher at school who'd noticed the bruises when I wore my gym clothes, but even she was too scared to get involved. Nobody in Boston wanted to deal with the mob and its people, especially guys like Dad and the men he brought home.

"Dad didn't exactly have a soft touch when it came to parenting - if you could even call what he did parenting."

"He beat you?"

"When I was around twelve, I started talking back, questioning the way he was doing things. At first, he'd just shout at me and lock me in my room until he felt like I'd been punished enough. But when I got a bit older, and he got a big drunker, he started to hit me when I'd speak up.

"At first, it wasn't too bad, and he'd apologize the next morning. Sometimes, he'd even buy me little gifts to make up for it. But then things escalated and by the time I was seventeen, he was kicking the shit out of me to make a point."

"Didn't anyone notice and help you?"

"One teacher tried to help, but eventually she stopped. I think Dad had threatened her family. He always made sure to hit and kick me where it wouldn't show. Never the face, but my shoulders, stomach, and thighs were his favorite places to bruise. He even once broke my wrist, but he told the doctor that I'd fallen out of a tree. I was sixteen and hadn't climbed a tree in years."

"What about your sister? Did he beat her too?"

"No, Riana was always a daddy's girl. She did exactly as she was told and turned a blind eye when he came after me. She only stood up to him one time but quickly changed her tune when he asked her if she wanted the same treatment."

"Fuck. I'm going to kill that man. I'm going to go to Boston, find that fucker, and tear him limb from limb."

Matteo was standing now, his voice filled with rage and his hands balled up at his sides.

"Don't waste your time. He's just a sad old man who nobody cares about anymore. The only person who gives him the time of day is my sister's husband, and that's because he married into the family. The deal he tried to make with the Sullivans was his way of getting some kind of respect; and that's obviously gone to shit since we told everyone I married you."

I got up and stood next to him, softly touching his hands and trying to get him to unclench them. It took a moment, but it worked. He visibly calmed as I massaged his hands with mine. It was an intimate movement, but it felt right in the moment. I didn't even think about what I was doing until my lips were touching his. The touch was featherlight and soft, nothing like the feverish kisses we'd shared before. At first, he didn't respond. He just let me kiss him. But when I ran my tongue across his bottom lip, he wrapped his arms around me and pulled me close.

We must have stood there in a tight embrace, kissing each other softly for ages. We didn't shift our position or try to get closer. It was sweet and sensual, like we had all the time in the world. For a while I waited for him to stop us and give me his little speech again. But he said nothing.

Eventually, Matteo took my hand and led me to the bed. He lay me down and kissed me deeply, moving his lips down my neck, my collar bone, my breasts, my stomach - shifting my nightgown down my body as we worked my skin with his lips. He slipped my underwear down, spreading my thighs and leaving soft open-mouthed kissed on my legs all the way down to the tops of my feet. Then, before I could move, he was up again, nipping and kissing the inside of my thighs.

By the time his hot, wet mouth focused on my core, I was more than ready for him. I cried out as he sucked my clit into his mouth and released it only to repeat the motion a few more times. He flattened his tongue, licking me from my dripping core to my sensitive nub and back again. He was taking his time. I almost wanted to beg him to speed up, but it felt too good, and I didn't want to ruin the moment.

When he stuck two fingers inside me and curled the rough digits, I squeezed my eyes shut, trying not to drown in the overwhelming pleasure. Just with his fingers and his talented tongue, I came so hard that I saw stars, and I didn't think I would ever come back down to earth. He carried on playing me like an instrument while I called out his name and rode out the high, my entire body shaking.

After that, he stood up and I watched him slowly take off his T-shirt and push down his sweatpants. He wasn't wearing underwear; his rock hard cock stood proud and tall as he made his way back to the bed. He gave himself long, slow strokes as he climbed on top of me and kissed me deeply. This time was so different from the first two times we'd had sex. The first time had been fun - we were celebrating and high from Vegas and the champagne. The second time had been desperate and feverish. This time, this time, it was slow and sweet. It was actually caring and intimate. He wanted to hold me, and I didn't want him to let me go.

I wrapped my legs around his waist, and he pushed himself all the way in with one swift movement and then stilled, so I could adjust to his size. At first, he was slow, taking his time, enjoying the joining of our two bodies. Eventually, we both couldn't take it anymore, and he sped up, with me meeting him thrust for thrust. We both came at the same time but refused to detangle our limbs from one another. We lay there in silence, both trying to catch our breaths.

He'd come inside me, but I didn't say anything. I'd gotten better at taking my birth control pills, and I didn't want to ruin the moment. That night he slept in my bed; and when I woke up, I was still wrapped up in his arms - both of us still naked. His eyes were already open and he kissed my forehead. I didn't want to move. I wanted to stay like that forever.

It felt right.

Chapter 10

MATTEO

♥

I woke at around nine am and just watched Arabella as she lay there sleeping, feeling the intimacy of her naked body in my arms. I couldn't remember the last time I'd ever slept that late, probably not since high school. I was usually such an early riser. But I couldn't stand the idea of leaving while she was sleeping, not again.

I had no awful speech planned for that morning. I wanted to wake up slowly with the beautiful woman in my arms and then have a leisurely breakfast with her. After that, I would call my brother and get him to take a little trip to Boston with me. Even though my brother had been a total asshole the day before, once I explained the situation and what Arabella's father had done, he'd be more than happy to take the trip I had planned.

Liam Flynn was going to meet his brand new son-in-law and see exactly how much I cared for his daughter, even if I hadn't told her that yet. At least I'd felt that I'd shown her I cared. There was no way she didn't know I had feelings for her after the way we'd slept together the night before. I'd never had sex like that before. I fucked, and I fucked hard. I liked sex, but it was never sweet and sensual. It was rough and exciting. What had happened the night before between the two of us felt...significant.

Once Arabella had woken up, we took a long, hot shower together. She tried to bring up the night before, but I kissed her until she dropped the subject. It wasn't that I didn't want to have that conversation; there were just things I wanted to do first. I made us breakfast while she got ready and then we ate together in a content silence. It was actually really nice. I'd never had a quiet breakfast with a woman before, where I wasn't trying to get her out of my apartment so I could go to work.

It was weird, I hadn't even thought about Gallbury Tech all that much since we'd been on our "honeymoon". Obviously, I still cared about the company, but I hadn't even opened my laptop to work from home during this time. Of course, family concerns had kept me busy the previous day and the day before that when we'd had to entertain Riana.

It felt good having something aside from Gallbury Tech and the Romano family. Something that was different and new and...special. Something, or rather someone, who I wanted to spend time with that had nothing to do with duty, responsibility, or money. I was about to announce that I'd be gone for the day and suggest that Arabella invite Brian over so for a redo of the night before - with my blessing and apologies this time. But her phone started ringing from her bedroom. She ignored it the first time, telling me she'd call whoever it was back. But then it rang again...and again.

I walked with her to her bedroom and watched as her face paled when she looked at the notification.

"Who was it?" I already knew the answer.

"My father. Don't worry I'm not going to answer it. I'm going to be strong this time, I promise."

"You don't have to promise me anything. This is about what's best for you, and only you know that. Having said that, I'm taking a trip to meet my new father-in-law today and let him know that if he continues to contact you, there will be consequences. I don't need your blessing, but I'd like it."

"Be careful. He doesn't look as dangerous as he is." That was all she said.

"And I don't look nearly as dangerous as I am. He won't be bothering you again. That I promise you."

With that, I went and got dressed, grabbing my gun and tucking it into the top of my pants. I didn't want things to get messy; but if they did, I wanted to be prepared. I wouldn't hesitate to put a bullet in that man's head if it meant that Arabella would remain safe.

I realized that there was very little I wouldn't do for Arabella's safety and happiness. What started out as helping my personal assistant get out of a sticky situation had ended in something entirely more meaningful. I grabbed my phone, kissed Arabella firmly on the lips, and then left the apartment. I called my brother in the elevator on the way down.

"I need your help."

"Ooh, say that again, I'm getting tingles." Clearly my brother was in a better mood than the day before.

"No time to joke about. We're heading out to Boston. I'll explain everything on the way."

·♥·♥·♥·♥·♥·

"What the fuck do you want?"

Liam answered the door shirtless in a pair of dirty jeans with a cigarette hanging from his mouth. Fuck, the man made me want to beat him senseless, and he hadn't even done anything yet. He just looked like the type of guy who would beat on his innocent daughter.

"Let me in. We've got some things to sort out."

"Like fucking hell I'm going to let you into my home. Fucking Romano asshole."

I moved my jacket aside to reveal my gun and he stepped aside.

"You think you're special coz you got a weapon. Son, every fucking Tom, Dick, and Harry in this town has a fucking weapon. You're lucky I don't give you a fucking whipping for being disrespectful."

"I'm not your daughter. I fight back and a lot harder than she ever would. I'll do what she's always dreamed of doing and put you in the fucking ground; then I'll spit on your grave and never think of you again. And not one motherfucker in the Sullivan family will give a shit that one of their errand boys got gunned down for being a piece of shit."

That's when things took a turn from verbal to physical. The old bastard tried to punch me in the face. But unlucky for him, I was quick on my feet. I turned, ducked out of the way, and hit him square in the jaw. Once it was clear I had the upper hand, he backed off a bit and took a beer out the fridge. I looked at my watch, it was after one pm, but that definitely wasn't his first drink of the day.

"So, what the fuck you want then?"

"I want you to leave my wife the fuck alone. I want you to forget that she was ever born. From now on you only have one daughter and you've never even heard of Arabella Romano."

"I don't know what the fuck makes her so special to you. She's weak. Always has been. She'll embarrass your family just like she's always embarrassed mine. I think the reason my wife died was because that bitch wife of yours was such an embarrassment to her."

After that, he couldn't say a word. I didn't think he'd be speaking to anyone for a while given the state of his face. My brother had to pull me off him and talk me out of putting a bullet in his head. In the end, the only reason Liam Flynn got to keep his life was because Arabella wouldn't want me committing a crime on her behalf. I already knew how much she hated the world we both lived in. I didn't want to make it worse for her.

· ♥ · ♥ · ♥ · ♥ · ♥ ·

I didn't go straight home. I was too wound up, wanting to take action. So, I used that energy and called together some of the most trusted Romanos. We all gathered in the backroom of my uncle's restaurant and talked about our strategy for revenge against the Sullivans. After all, they'd dared to go after our territory.

My cousins, father, and brother all agreed that we'd set targeted attacks on their warehouses over the next few weeks. Every time they thought it was over, they would start to recover what they'd lost, but it would start all over again. It was about sending a message, and it was going to be loud and clear.

Don't fuck with the Romanos, and definitely don't fuck with Arabella Romano.

I could tell my father was proud of the action I was taking, but the last thing I wanted was for him to think this was my way of saying I was ready to take over the family business. I knew that I was in it for life because of blood, but I would put off that responsibility for as long as I possibly could. I was proud to be a Romano, but I also had other plans in life.

I decided to have a conversation with him about it soon. We hadn't really sat down to discuss the future of the Romano family since I was a teenager. Everyone just assumed that I would be next in line. But if there was a chance that my brother would take over, I wanted to explore it with my father. Of course, you never truly leave a crime family as rooted and ingrained as the Romano family was in the mafia. But if there was a way to stay close to my parents and siblings and still have my own life, I wanted to at least see what I could do to make that happen.

Arabella didn't want to be with a man who lived that kind of life. I didn't blame her after seeing what she grew up with. I'd hoped that by then, she knew I wasn't like the man who had "raised" her, but how could she be certain that I wouldn't change after a few drinks. I needed to figure out what I was going to do with my life and how I was going to manage it all. But at that particular moment, I just wanted to go home to Arabella and maybe have a quiet dinner with the woman who was pretending to be my wife.

It may not have been real, but I could enjoy her while she was around.

· ♥ · ♥ · ♥ · ♥ · ♥ ·

"What happened today?" Arabella was waiting for me in the kitchen when I got home. She was cooking something on the stove that smelt absolutely amazing.

"Let's just say that your father won't be contacting you ever again. Not unless he's even fucking more stupid than he already looks."

"Do I want to know the details?"

"You don't need to know the details. But if you ever really want to know something, just ask and I will be completely honest with you. I trust you to keep my secrets, and I want you to trust me to always put your best interests first."

For a second, it looked like she wanted to say something, but then she turned back to the pot on the stove and pulled out a spoon filled with meat and a thick sauce.

"Taste this." She put the spoon to my lips.

I leaned forward and tasted the food. It was spectacular.

"I didn't know you could cook?"

"I'm full of surprises. This is an old Irish stew recipe from my grandmother. I've adapted it a bit over the years, but it's essentially an old family recipe."

We sat and ate dinner and talked at length about Arabella's grandmother. I made a mental note of every detail because I knew this woman was clearly someone important in Arabella's life. I thought that maybe I'd surprise her with a trip to Ireland once the whole thing with the Sullivans had been sorted out.

Chapter 11

ARABELLA

♥

As I watched Matteo eat the Irish stew I'd made from my grandmother's recipe, I'd gotten a little too deep. He was a great guy, and I was starting to see that only too clearly. He was loving, family-orientated, fiercely loyal, and committed to doing what he thought was the right thing. But that didn't change the fact that he was a criminal.

He wasn't just a petty criminal doing odd jobs to survive; no, he was part of the biggest and most successful crime family in New York City. He was a billionaire in his own right and didn't need the money at all. He was a criminal because that's what he was raised to be. He was in too deep, and from what I'd seen, he wasn't about to denounce his family.

No, I couldn't fall for him. I knew that deep in my gut. But, at the same time, I couldn't help melting when

I thought of how tenderly he'd held me the night before, and how sweet and caring he'd been. The fact that he'd gone to see my dad proved that he gave a shit about me.

I wasn't used to having people care so much about my happiness. At least, not since my mother had been alive. I knew that Grandmother cared - she cared a lot - but she was all the way in Ireland. My sister had been more interested in getting Dad's positive attention - which he always reserved for her. And Father only gave a shit about me when it came to getting what he wanted.

When dinner was over, Matteo helped me clear up and offered to pour me another glass of wine. I really wanted to accept it and ease into the night. Hopefully, it would end with both of us naked. That was a bad idea and I needed to start making good decisions, especially where my heart was concerned.

"I think I'm just going to head to bed and get some much-needed sleep."

"Alright then, have a good night." He smiled and gave me a peck on the cheek. I could tell that he was a little disappointed. I hated that I'd made him feel that way.

By the time I reached my bedroom, I wanted to turn around and go straight back to him. I didn't want to sleep alone in my bed, which still had his unique masculine scent all over the sheets. I closed my door softly instead and began to get undressed. I didn't sleep particularly well, I kept tossing and turning, thinking about what to do about my situation. I couldn't possibly stay with Matteo forever, but the second I ended our "marriage", my father would come after me to marry into the Sullivan family. I knew that for certain.

When I was able to sleep, I dreamed about how awful my life would be back in Boston. The inevitable beatings by my drunk husband, the constant disrespect, and the fact that I definitely wouldn't be allowed to have a job. I'd just be there to serve men and create the next generation of Sullivan degenerates. I couldn't think of anything worse.

Yes, I wanted to be a mother, but I didn't want to be a mother in a criminal organization, let alone one as abusive to women as the Sullivans were. That was another reason I needed to sort out the situation with Matteo.

We weren't really married, and we weren't even in a relationship. I didn't know what we were. At some point, I'd want to meet someone (not involved in the criminal lifestyle) and have my own family. I couldn't do that or couldn't even date, while I was in a fake marriage with Matteo Romano.

Don't get me wrong, I was definitely grateful for everything he'd done for me. If it weren't for him and his family connections, I'd be married in Boston with a life sentence that I had absolutely no say in. I would be completely stuck. He'd saved me, and I was thankful for it. But it didn't mean that I wanted to spend the rest of my life like this.

·♥·♥·♥·♥·♥·

The next morning, I got up at around seven am, even though I was exhausted. I couldn't sleep and didn't want any more restless nightmares about the Sullivans and what my life could have been if Matteo had not come along. I washed my face and brushed my teeth before going into the kitchen, just in case Matteo was still around.

He was sitting at the kitchen counter, sipping coffee like he hadn't slept well, either. But damn, he looked gorgeous in his gray sweatpants and a white T-shirt that perfectly showed off his muscular physique. Even with his hair all messy and stubble on his face, he looked like he could be in an ad for some fancy coffee brand. I could picture him sitting on a billboard in Times Square.

"Morning, how'd you sleep?" His voice was gruff, and it stirred something deep inside me. It took all my self-control not to walk up to him and put my hands all over him.

"Not great. Too much going on in my head, I guess. And you? Did you get some sleep?" From the look of him, I knew that he hadn't. But I didn't want to say that out loud.

"Same my side. Do you want to order in some breakfast? Or we could go out?"

The thought of getting showered and dressed to go out for breakfast seemed like too much to do on very little sleep. I also didn't see the need to order breakfast in, when we had a fully stocked fridge.

"Don't worry about it, I'll make us breakfast. We have everything for a nice fry up."

"You know I don't expect you to cook for me. You don't owe me anything, and I certainly don't expect you to take care of me. I'm not that kind of guy."

I smiled. "I know you're not. I actually enjoy cooking for you. Your kitchen is amazing. The kitchen in my old apartment was the worst; you could barely move in it. This one has everything I could need. I could spin around with my arms extended and not hit a thing. I love it."

"Well then, if you love it, who am I to stop you?" He winked, and I swear I could feel my heart flutter. I tried my best to shove that feeling as deep down as I could. I didn't want to have such a reaction.

I kicked him out of the kitchen to go take a shower while I cooked. I played some music from the sound system and got into the rhythm of it, dancing while frying up eggs, sausages, and strips of bacon. I stuck some bread in the toaster and got jam and honey from the pantry. For someone who ordered in and ate out a lot, he had a fully-stocked pantry and fridge. By the time he came back from his shower, the food was ready.

This time, he was wearing a pair of fitted blue jeans and a black tee, looking delectable with his damp hair. The lingering scent of his cologne nearly made me pass out. I wanted to walk around the kitchen counter and taste him. I knew better. In fact, I needed to talk to him about finding a long-term solution to my problem. We couldn't pretend to be married for the rest of our lives. Even if I was okay with being tied to a crime family like the Romanos, it wasn't fair to expect him to put his life on hold for me.

I waited until we were finished eating before I broached the subject. "We need to talk."

"Oh shit, that doesn't sound good." There was a slight chuckle in his voice, but I could tell that he was concerned.

"We can't carry on like this. We need to find a real solution."

He groaned and raked his hand through his hair. "Yeah, I know, living like this is really asking a lot of you, isn't it." His voice was thick with sarcasm, and I wasn't expecting it.

"That's not what I meant. I appreciate everything you've done for me, but I can't just spend my life pretending to be your wife."

"Yeah, must fucking suck, living in a penthouse apartment in the Upper East Side, with your every need taken care of." He stood up, turning his back to me as he took his plate to the sink.

I put my hand on his shoulder, trying to calm him down. "You know I don't mean that. But this isn't a long-term solution. We should both be free to live our lives."

"You think I haven't been fucking trying? You think I'm trying to keep you here against you will. Think about it, Arabella. I've been doing all I can. All you want is to get as far away from me as possible."

His tone was downright hostile, and I flinched as he turned around sharply to face me. He took a step back, realizing that he'd startled me again.

"Fuck!" He hit the counter with a closed fist. "You still think I'm going to harm you? What do I have to do to prove myself to you?"

"I don't..." He didn't even listen to my response, storming off to his bedroom and slamming the door.

I did the dishes with tears streaming down my face. The talk hadn't gone the way I'd planned. I'd meant to thank him, tell him how grateful I was, and then ask what we were going to do. The last thing I'd wanted was to end up fighting with him. It didn't feel right to carry on putting him through all my shit, especially after I'd insulted him like that. I also didn't appreciate the way he'd spoken to me. I needed to get out of that apartment. I'd figure out my next move once I had the space to think properly.

I went to my room and packed a bag. I only took the essentials. I could send someone to get the rest of my things once everything had settled down. I couldn't stand all the fighting. I didn't want to be a burden on him anymore, even though he'd never said that I was.

I only knew one person in New York who I could go to. I just hoped that he was home and willing to let me sleep on his sofa until I figured out my next move. I moved so fast that I probably packed my bag in less than ten minutes. If Matteo had time to calm down, he'd apologize, and we'd probably end up naked again.

·♥·♥·♥·♥·♥·

"Well, shit, come in and take a load off, sweetie." Brian didn't even ask why I was standing there, with puffy eyes and a week's worth of clothing in a suitcase. He just welcomed me in and offered me a margarita, even though it wasn't even eleven am yet. After the morning I'd had, I considered it for a moment before requesting a cup of coffee instead.

I spent the rest of the day on Brian's sofa, telling him the full story about my life, my father's deal, and how Matteo had helped me out, and I'd ruined everything. He even comforted me while I cried. We ordered in Chinese and put on a sappy movie. He said it was so we didn't waste our tears on a man.

Chapter 12
MATTEO

♥

I came out of my bedroom and went to knock on Arabella's door, but it was already open and she was nowhere to be found. I searched the rest of the apartment; she had clearly gone out. I tried calling her, but her cellphone went straight to voicemail. I didn't bother leaving a message. Instead, I texted her, saying how sorry I was and that I shouldn't have reacted the way I did.

When she hadn't responded or come home by eight pm, I was more than concerned. I had no idea whether she was safe or not. I didn't know where she was and was worried out of my mind. I decided to check her bedroom for any clues.

When I checked the bathroom, her toothbrush and beauty products were missing. Upon closer inspection, I noticed that her suitcase and half her clothes were gone. I went through the entire apartment to make sure that she hadn't left me a note. After that, I must have called her about 1000 times, but it kept going to voicemail.

I called my father and explained the situation. He was the only one who really knew the truth, so it made sense to get his help. He promised that he'd call a few of his most trusted guys and get them to help me search the city until we found her. He told me that he was going to tell Mother that it was business so she wouldn't start to worry.

I agreed and told him to keep it from my sisters. The last thing I wanted was the whole family freaked out because I'd gone and lost my shit for no reason. Why did I have to be such a fucking asshole?

I knew why I'd reacted like that. I didn't want Arabella to leave and we couldn't be a long-term thing. She wanted a life far away from crime, and I was a member of the Romano family. Nothing would change that. I couldn't give her what she ultimately wanted. But that didn't mean that I could just cut off my feelings.

In such a short period of time, that woman had snuck her way into my whole system. I wanted to be around her constantly. I didn't just want to fuck her - although the sex was life-changing - I also wanted to talk late into the night with her and wake up and have breakfast with her the next morning.

Most of all, I wanted her to be safe. I couldn't make sure of that while I didn't have any idea where she was. If only I hadn't been such a giant asshole . I knew exactly why she had flinched when I came toward her too quickly. I should have apologized, but I hated the fact that she still didn't feel completely safe from harm with me. It wasn't her fault. None of this was her fault ,yet I'd acted like it was.

I swore that if I found her safe and sound, I'd make a bigger effort to be a decent guy. I would do whatever I needed to get her back in my apartment safe and sound. I would find a solution that didn't involve having to be married to a Romano. As long as she was okay, I would do anything to ensure she was never in harm's way again.

According to my private investigator, Arabella had no family in the city, which I already knew. I could only think of one friend; it was that guy who'd been at my apartment when I'd freaked out at her after a long day. I promised myself I would stop losing my shit. She didn't deserve it.

I'd just been a hard-ass for so long that I'd forgotten how to be a softer version of myself, one that a woman like Arabella could feel comfortable around. I had a lot of work to do, but I'd do it as long as I could make sure she was safe. I would change my behavior...even if it meant giving her up in the long run. I'd do what was best for her. I just needed to get her home where I could watch over her.

At around nine pm, I got a call, giving me Brian's address. One of my father's men was already on his way there. I told him to just confirm that she was there and then keep an eye out - but not go near her. I didn't want to freak her out by having one of the Romano soldiers bring her back to me. No, I needed to go over there myself and convince her to come back.

The apartment was in the same building that Arabella had lived in previously, which was in a shitty part of town (not the worst, but not even close to being the best). I had my guy keep an eye out at the entrance to make sure no one from the Sullivan family found her. Not that they knew that she'd left my place; but it was best to be sure.

It took thirty minutes to get there. It felt like the longest half an hour of my entire life. I was fidgeting in my seat the whole journey. I almost punched the driver when he tried to make small talk. Again, it was that type of behavior I needed to change if I wanted to keep Arabella around...at least until I could guarantee her safety and freedom.

I leapt out of the car when I saw the apartment building and ran up the three flights of stairs to Brian's place. I was about to pound on the door when I realized that I needed to calm down. I needed to speak to her without being a demanding asshole. I couldn't just pick her up and carry her home. She had to come willingly.

Eventually, I knocked on the door - a bit too softly at first, then a little more firmly to get their attention. I could hear the television through the door, meaning they were probably watching a movie. Which was good, it meant that she was okay. I almost felt bad for interrupting their evening.

"The fuck do you want?" Arabella had clearly been confiding in her best friend because he was not pleased to see me.

"I just want to talk to her. That's all. I won't cause any shit, I promise." I was moments away from pleading with the guy...or physically moving him out of my way - whatever it took.

"Give me one good reason why I should let you see her? She's been sitting in my living room crying all day, and I've finally got her to relax a bit. Why should I let you disrupt all that progress?"

"Has she told you the full story?"

"Yes, I know everything. I know that you did her a solid, but that doesn't mean you get to be a dickhead to her."

"I know. I get that and I promise I'll be better. But I have a good reason for being here. I can protect her from her dad, from the Sullivans, and whatever comes her way. Being with me gives her protection. You can't offer her that."

"Just because you can keep her safe doesn't mean you can be a total asshole. She deserves to be treated like a human being. No, fuck that, she deserves to be treated better than the average human being because she's a truly great person. Can you do that? Because if you can't, then I'm going to have to ask you to leave."

We both knew that he couldn't realistically get me to leave. It's not like he could call the cops on me. I was a Romano; we had so many cops in our pocket that we basically ran the local police force. But if I wanted to get through to Arabella, I needed to get through to her friend first.

"Look, I just want to see her and make sure that she's safe. You and I have the same intention: we want her to be happy. I promise that if you let me talk to her, I'll leave her alone if she wants me to. I'll set up some of my guys in the building so she's protected, and I'll never contact her again."

I didn't know if I could go through with that promise, but I was counting on gaining Arabella's forgiveness.

"Fine, come in." Brian moved aside, allowing me to enter his apartment.

Arabella was lying on his couch, her cheeks tear-stained and her eyes puffy and red from crying. I felt like the world's greatest idiot. Of course, she still looked beautiful. I don't think I'd ever seen her when she wasn't completely stunning.

"I'll let you two talk. But remember that I'm just in the next room. Shout if you need me, Bella."

She sat up, wiping at her face, trying to right herself. I took a seat opposite her and breathed deeply. I'd need to make the speech of all speeches to make it up to her.

"I behaved terribly. I should never have spoken to you that way. You deserve so much better. I know that you just want your life back, I completely understand that and would feel the same way if I was in your shoes."

I took a deep breath, watching her sitting there, waiting for a further explanation.

"You've been treated like shit by too many people for far too long. So, I get why you needed to get away from me. But I promise that I'll be better. I won't ever speak to you like that again. I'm just so used to being alone that I don't know how to show how much I care without being an asshole. I know it's not right, and I don't have an excuse.

"I know that pretending to be married just means that you're dependent on another crime family. I know that you feel trapped and under my thumb. So, I'm going to find a solution to this whole mess. A way for you to live independently and not be harassed by your father and the Sullivans.

"But I need time. This is a delicate situation, and if I show any weakness where you're concerned, they're going to take advantage of it. I couldn't fucking handle it if anything happened to you. Right now, they're pissed and ready to start a war with me and my family. We've got a plan to put them in their place. All I need is a bit of time. After that, I promise to let you go and live your life.

"Until then, I need you to come home with me. It's the only way that I can make sure you're okay. I couldn't live with myself if something happened to you because I don't know how to behave myself. I care about you. I care about you a lot...and I'll do whatever it takes to protect you."

I finally stopped speaking and watched as she stared back at me, clearly thinking things through. There was nothing more that I could say. What happened next was completely up to her. If she told me to leave, I would have no choice. She cleared her throat, and I waited for her response. My heart was beating so fast that I was pretty sure Brian could hear it from where he was obviously eavesdropping.

Chapter 13

ARABELLA

♥

I thought about my response for a few heavy moments before replying. Matteo needed to know that I didn't take this decision lightly. This was my future - and I guess his as well - and I had to know that I would be safe with him. The thing was, I didn't doubt for a second that under his protection, I would be okay. I felt it deep inside me. He would do whatever it took to make sure that I wasn't in harm's way.

"I'll come home with you because I truly believe you have my best interests at heart. But I need to know that you'll do everything in your power to help me find another solution. You're a good man, Matteo, but I can't be involved in your world. I refuse to go back to a life so intimately connected with the underbelly of society."

"I understand. But you have to understand that I'm not like them; I'm nothing like the men you grew up with.

I wouldn't hurt you and neither would anyone in my family. But I get why you feel the way you do, and I'll do everything I can to help you find a solution that keeps you safe and gets you out of the criminal world."

He stood up, extending his hand to me. I accepted it and stood up to go with him.

"Just give me a few minutes to say goodbye to Brian."

"Yeah, no worries, I'll be outside waiting for you. Just yell if you need me."

I couldn't imagine why I'd need him when he was just being protective. Something inside me liked that he cared so much about me. As much as I wanted to get away from his world, I didn't hate the way he made me feel. In all honesty, I enjoyed it. I liked feeling...cherished.

"I swear to god if you don't marry that man, I will," Brian theatrically whispered to me as soon as the door shut behind Matteo.

"That's not an option and I've told you why. I can't be involved in that lifestyle. I won't be put in that position."

"Honey, with the way that man looks, he could put me in any position he wanted."

I playfully smacked Brian's arm. "Thank you for being there for me today, I really appreciate it. I had nowhere else to go, and you welcomed me into your home. I'll never forget that. Thank you."

"You're always welcome here. But, if I were you, I'd enjoy living in a penthouse apartment with that hottie billionaire. I'm always here if he misbehaves again."

I gave Brian a solid hug and he kept me there for a minute. "Thank you for telling me everything. I'm here if you need me and I mean that."

· ♥ · ♥ · ♥ · ♥ · ♥ ·

I was exhausted by the time we got back to Matteo's apartment. After the terrible sleep we'd both had the night before, it was clear that we needed to rest, especially after such an emotion-filled day. But somehow, we both lingered in the kitchen, not wanting to go our separate ways.

"There's something I haven't told you - something I need you to know." His voice was low and serious. I couldn't take it anymore that day, but I needed to hear him out. Whatever it was, I would have to deal with it, and I'd rather know sooner than later. I didn't want any surprises. Surprises were never good.

"Tell me, I'm listening." My heart sped up, and I felt my stomach tighten.

"I make a mean hot chocolate. Honestly, it'll be the best you've ever had. I'm sorry for keeping this secret from you. I won't do it again."

I exhaled and even giggled a little. "You'll have to prove it to me. It's not that I don't believe you, I believe that *you* think you make the best hot chocolate, but I've had some damn good hot chocolate in my time."

I took a seat, and he moved deeper into the kitchen, taking ingredients out of the cupboards and putting a pot on the stove. The air suddenly felt a lot lighter, and I was relieved. Things had been so tense, and I could use a moment of simple ease between us.

We drank hot chocolate in the living room, draped over the sofa, relaxing as best we could. My eyes were drifting shut by the time I had finished my last sip. But I still didn't want to go to bed and leave him. And even though it was a terrible idea, I wanted to be with him. Not in a sexual way (I was too exhausted to even think of sex): I just enjoyed his company.

He put his hot chocolate down on the table and pulled my bare foot into his lap. He began to slowly massage it. I groaned because it felt so damn good, and he grinned in response. I lay still as he went to work. I don't know when I fell asleep, but when I woke up, I was alone in my bed. I was still fully dressed. I appreciated that Matteo hadn't changed me without my knowledge. It was important to me that he valued my consent in everything we did together.

I got changed into a T-shirt and brushed my teeth, then went straight back to sleep. We were due back at the office the next day. When I'd left, I'd planned to leave my job. It wasn't like I could run away from him and then just go back to work like everything was normal. But after returning home with him, I figured it made sense to still work for him. It would be weird if I didn't.

I woke up at six am and decided to get up and make us both breakfast before we went to the office. By the time I reached the kitchen, Matteo was already there - half naked and making an omelet. I gawked at his sculpted body for a little too long before he noticed that I was there and gave me a knowing smile.

Fuck. I'd been caught staring. Oh well, it wasn't like he didn't know I was attracted to him.

"I was just getting ready to make you breakfast, but you beat me to it."

"Yeah well, if you thought my hot chocolate was good, you need to try my omelets. There aren't many dishes I can cook well, but I make a killer loaded omelet. Sit your ass down and let me serve you for once."

My temperature spiked a little at the demanding tone in his voice, and I did as I was told. I usually wasn't a fan of people, especially the men in my life telling me what to do. But this was different. Maybe it was due to him wearing nothing but a pair of sweatpants (black for a change).

"Are you ready to get back to the office? Honestly, I'm a bit surprised you survived this long without being there. You're usually quite hands-on at work."

"You think I'm controlling?"

"No, I think you're...passionate. You care about the business. It's obvious that you've invested a lot of time and energy into it. I can't believe you stayed away for so long."

"Well, if that surprised you, what I'm going to say next is totally going to shock your socks off."

"Shock my socks off? That's an interesting turn of phrase." I was giggling as he handed me my omelet, and I started to dig into it.

"Can we go five minutes without you mouthing off at me?" He raised an eyebrow but was chuckling under his breath. "I was just thinking that maybe we could take one more day off from work. I thought we could play hooky today, line up some movies, get some snacks, and veg out in front of the TV."

I couldn't have thought of anything better. It was raining outside, and the last thing I wanted was to venture to the office, where there would surely be a million questions waiting for me about how I'd ended up marrying my boss. It was inevitable that I'd go back, but one day of peace wouldn't be the worst thing. After all, the previous day had been a little hellish.

"That sounds delightful...what movies are you thinking of?"

"I thought it would be a cool idea to show each other our favorite movies. I already have my top two picked out."

"Let me guess, The Godfather one and two?" I giggled as he swatted at me with a dishtowel.

"Not, I'm not nearly that cliche."

"Top Gun and Die Hard?"

"Fuck, you've got me there." I laughed out loud at his admission.

"Fine, I'm happy to sit through your tough guy movies, as long as we can watch my favorites."

"Let me guess, Pretty Woman and The Notebook."

"Not even close. You've got me all wrong Mr. Romano."

"Well then what are your top picks for this rainy movie day? I need to know, so I can line them up."

"The Shining and The Princess Diaries." I couldn't help but laugh at the expression on his face.

"I don't know what to be more disturbed by? The fact that you're a thriller fan or that one of your favorite movies was made for pre-teens who dreamed of being princesses?"

"You should definitely be more disturbed by the latter. I'm still waiting for my grandmother to tell me I'm the heir to the throne of a small European country I've never even heard of."

We finished our omelets (he was right, he did make a mean loaded omelet) and then we headed into the living room armed with blankets, still in the (very few) clothes we'd slept in. At least I'd put on a pair of pajama shorts before going into the kitchen. Matteo was still refusing to wear a shirt, but there was no way I was going to complain. Not when he had that sexy V-thing I'd only seen on models and actors.

The rest of the day was probably one of the loveliest days I'd ever had in my life. I'd never really had days like that at home - days that were peaceful and relaxed. If I'd ever just spent the day on the sofa at home, Dad would have killed me. I was there to serve him and his friend, cooking and cleaning was what I was made for.

It wasn't like I'd had the time to loll on the sofa since I'd been working. When I hadn't been at the office, I'd been maximizing my free time in the city, sightseeing and trying to take in all the perks of the freedom I'd never taken for granted.

It was amazing to just spend the day without a care in the world. And the company was the best part. As much as he'd complained about watching The Princess Diaries, he was just as invested in the future of Genovia as I was. I even enjoyed watching Die Hard and Top Gun; although I had seen them before, it was different watching them with Matteo.

I liked the way he chuckled at all the quippy one-liners. It was the hottest thing I'd ever heard if I were to be honest. The way his low voice rumbled through his chest and his mouth twitched at the sides was sexy and endearing all at once.

I could honestly have lived that day a thousand times and never gotten tired of it. I felt content... possibly for the first time in my entire life. Something about the simplicity of the two of us curled up on the sofa made my heart sing.

Chapter 14

MATTEO

♥

The day I played hooky with Arabella was one of the most amazing days of my life up till that point. And that's saying a lot. I never thought I could feel that good just sitting on the sofa watching The Princess Diaries and eating junk food. I couldn't remember the last time I'd spent that much time in one place, doing absolutely no work - not family business and nothing to do with Gallbury Tech.

It was all because of her. There was something truly special about Arabella Flynn, and I knew deep down that I would never meet anyone else as beautiful - both inside and out. The last thing I wanted was to let that woman go. But I didn't exactly have a choice. As much as I'd believed that I wanted to be alone, or at least not committed to someone until I had my future planned, I didn't want to let Arabella go. I had to, but when that day came, it would be one of the worst days of my life. I was sure of it.

No, what I needed to do was find a solution to the Sullivan problem just like I'd promised. Then I'd find a way to convince her to stay with me. I didn't want what was happening between us to be fake anymore: I wanted her for real, but it would have to be her decision. She needed to want to stay with me.

There were so many obstacles between us, but I was willing to blast each one out of the way. Would you want to do the same? My family was one of the reasons she didn't want to be attached to me. I loved my family. Despite being a criminal organization, they were good people, and I loved them. Maybe she'd come to see them as I did.

The next morning, I was tempted to suggest that we play hooky again. But we couldn't recreate that one perfect day. Besides, if you get too much of a good thing, it loses that something that makes it special. No, we had to go to work. It was such a weird feeling to be dreading going to the office. I usually couldn't wait to get up, get dressed, and get to work. That morning, however, I lingered in the kitchen, waiting for Arabella so we could go in together. I didn't even mind that she was running late. Anyway, it would have looked weird if we showed up at separate times. After all, she was my wife, according to the rest of the world.

Eventually, she came through looking gorgeous as always. There was a certain spring in her step. I swear that she looked even hotter in that office-safe pencil skirt than she had the last time I'd seen in it. I wanted to flip it up over her ass and pull down her panties. I shook my head to get my thoughts straight. The last thing I wanted was to walk into the office with a massive erection that wouldn't go down.

"I'm sorry I'm running late. I know how early you like to get to the office. I just need two sips of this coffee, and then I'm ready to go."

"Don't worry about it. I have an in with the boss." I winked at her. "I'm sure he won't mind if you stop for a quick bite on the way to the office."

She giggled; the sound was better than my favorite song.

· ♥ · ♥ · ♥ · ♥ · ♥ ·

After stopping at a diner for a quick stack of pancakes, we made it into the office around nine am. If anyone noticed, they didn't say anything. In fact, people were purposefully not looking at us. I'm pretty sure someone sent out a memo telling them not to make a big deal about us returning to work. I guess that's one of the perks of being the CEO: nobody wants to upset you or your brand new wife.

Arabella set her stuff down on her desk, and I went into my office and opened up my laptop for the first time since leaving for Vegas. The company hadn't gone bankrupt or burned down, so that was a massive positive. All in all, everything looked like it was on track.

At ten am, I decided to walk to the breakroom to get myself some coffee. It didn't feel right to ask Arabella to do it. It was such a little task that I could surely do it myself. As soon as I saw her in that skirt, talking to one of the other assistants, I wanted to pull her into my office and bend her over my desk. Again, I had to shake away the thought of her naked and begging me to fuck her. Instead, I made her coffee as well and stopped at her desk on the way back.

"What's this?" She looked up as I placed the mug down on her desk.

"What do you think it is?"

"I thought you said you were going to stop being an asshole?" Her words were harsh, but she was smiling and there was a glint in her eyes.

"I didn't think making you a cup of coffee made me an asshole, but I can go throw it down the drain if that would make you happy?"

"No, thank you. But you know making coffee is my job, right?"

"Your job is to do exactly what I want you to do. Right now, I need to speak to you in my office."

I turned my back to her swiftly, leaving her to follow me. I was happier than ever that no one could see into my office. Some of the senior executives had decided on glass walls to seem more transparent while I'd gone with solid walls to ensure my privacy. I hated the idea of being watched. And as I watched my pretend wife walk in after me, I couldn't have been more sure that I'd made the right decision.

"Close the door, Arabella." My voice was firm, commanding. I didn't care who might've heard me order my fake wife around.

She gave me a funny look, but still turned around and closed the door.

"Anything else I can do for you, sir?" Her voice was sexy and sultry. She was well aware why I'd called her into my office.

"Yes, bend yourself over my desk. I want to see your tits pushed flat against the wood, ass in the air."

She clearly didn't object to the dirty talk because she did exactly as she was told. I took my time walking up behind her. I leaned over to nuzzle her neck. I raked my hands from behind her knees all the way up her thighs, until I was lifting her skirt and bunching it up around her waist.

I knelt down behind her, biting her delicious ass through her silk panties. She let out a small gasp; but other than that, she didn't say anything. I took that as my cue to carry on. I slid my thumbs underneath her panties on either side, pulling them down until they were around her ankles.

Then I spread her legs, breathing in her glorious scent. She was already glistening from arousal, letting me know that she was enjoying it just as much as I was. I licked her from her swollen nub all the way to her core, angling her ass so I could sink my tongue in as deep as possible. Her resulting moan got me rock hard.

I then replaced my tongue with two fingers, moving in a rhythmic motion, speeding up to be in sync with her breathing. I bit her ass again as I circled her clit with my thumb, increasing my speed again. It didn't take long before she was panting and begging for more. I waited until her whole body was shaking before I stood up and took a step back, admiring the view - all open for me and needy with desire. I unbuckled my belt, pulled my erection out and gave myself a few slow strokes before stepping forward.

I grabbed her hips, lifting her to give me the perfect entrance. At this angle, I was able to get as deep as possible. I gave her a few seconds to adjust and then I started fucking her. I didn't bother going slow at first and working my way up. I was like a rabid animal.

Her moans started getting so loud that I was sure someone outside the office would hear her. I paused to pick up her panties from the floor and shove them in her mouth. Soon after, I could feel her come as her tight pussy constricted around me. I didn't let up, fucking her through her orgasm. Only then did I allow myself to come.

She spat out the panties and grinned at me. "That was fucking life-changing." I grinned in response and used the panties to clean my cum, which was sliding down her thighs.

I was about to suggest round two when a harsh knock came from the door, snapping us back to reality.

"Fuck off!"

"Mr. Romano, the board is waiting for you. You had a meeting scheduled for ten minutes. I don't know where Miss Flynn is, but she should have put it in your schedule."

"Shit," Arabella whispered under her breath.

"Mrs. Romano!"

"What, sir?"

"You called her Miss Flynn. Her name is Arabella Romano, in case you didn't get the memo."

I tucked myself in, zipped up my pants, and buckled my belt. "I'll be there in two minutes. I'm very busy." I shot a smirk at Arabella.

Once the helpful assistant of one of my colleagues had fucked off, I told Arabella to take her time getting herself together before going there. Then I opened my office door and strode to the board meeting.

It was the usual shit. Investors getting greedy and wanted higher returns. I told them we'd made them more than enough money, and they were welcome to pull their investments if it wasn't satisfactory. Then one of the senior executives made up for my brash attitude by sucking up to the assholes. It was the same fucking shit I'd dealt with a thousand times over.

I spent the majority of the meeting replaying what had happened in my office only moments before while trying not to get hard while still in the boardroom. We must have been in there for two or more hours because food was delivered by one of the assistants. We took a break to eat, but I didn't have much of an appetite.

I spent the rest of the day in multiple meetings, trying not to think about all the ways I wanted to fuck Arabella. The woman was more addictive than any drug I'd ever heard of. If I could spend the rest of my life making her scream, I'd be the happiest man alive.

That night, Arabella and I had lazy, sensual sex, and then fell asleep in my bed. I decided right then and there that I would make her mine, permanently. I would find her a way out of my life and then make sure she chose me instead. I wasn't above begging when it came to that woman.

I would have done anything to make her happy. I was certain of it. I would make sure that she never had a bad day for the rest of her life. Her shitty dad may have made the first part of her life hell, but I would spend the rest of mine making sure that she woke up every morning with a sleepy smile.

Chapter 15

ARABELLA

I don't know what had happened that led to that scene in Matteo's office, but I wanted it to happen again and again. I didn't think I'd ever get tired of him and his body. The man sure knew how to treat a woman. It was the best sex I'd ever had, and I couldn't get enough of him.

For the following two weeks, we acted like horny teenagers. Whether we were at the office, in the car (thank fuck for dividers), in the elevator, or in his apartment, we were constantly all over each other. It was completely amazing. I mean, I'd had sex before, but never like that. I'd never felt so needy and so satisfied at the same time. The few guys I'd slept with before were sloppy and only cared about their own enjoyment. Matteo wasn't like that. He gave me everything when we were naked together.

The moments in between were pretty damn great as well. As much as I didn't want to be involved in his world, being with him was truly something special. When Matteo gave me his full attention, I felt my heart start to enlarge. I even stopped asking him about how the search for a solution to my problem was going.

It wasn't that I wasn't going to leave him when I had the all clear. It was just that, honestly, I didn't want our time together to end. The problem was that I wanted a full life with a family - and peace and safety. I couldn't have that with him. I'd always be worried about whether he'd come home unharmed every night and whether our kids would be targeted because of who their dad was.

I had to leave him eventually, but that was something I was avoiding thinking about. Until a Tuesday morning two weeks later. I woke up feeling like I'd been hit by a truck. It was worse than the nastiest hangover I'd ever had, which was after far too many tequila shots with Brian. I hadn't even had a drink the night before. Matteo and I had been too distracted by each other to worry about alcohol.

Matteo had gone to the gym for an hour (which I realized was how he kept his amazing physique) and I'd stayed in bed to get more sleep. I relied on genetics and the odd run to maintain my figure. By the time he returned, I thought I was going to die.

He didn't want to go to work. He wanted to stay home with me to make sure I was okay. But I was feeling disgusted and didn't really want him to see me like that. So, eventually, I convinced him to go into the office, despite his arguing that he could work from home and keep an eye on me at the same time.

As soon as I heard the private elevator shut behind him, I ran to the bathroom and threw up. I'd been feeling nauseous all morning, but the last thing I wanted was my hot fake husband to see me empty the contents of my stomach into the toilet bowl. Once I started, I couldn't stop. When I felt like I had nothing left to puke, I went to the bedroom to grab a blanket. Then I ran back to the bathroom to throw up again. I wrapped the blanket around my shivering body and lay on the hard tiled floor.

For the next few hours, I drifted in and out of consciousness, throwing up and then falling asleep again. I was in absolute hell. I'd never felt this bad before in my entire life. It felt worse than the food poisoning I'd had after eating dinner at a one-star restaurant in Boston on a terrible date in high school. (To be fair, I hadn't known it was a one-star restaurant when I'd agreed to go).

Finally, I stopped throwing up; there was honestly nothing left inside, and my ribs were sore from dry heaving. I was too exhausted and weak to make it back to the bed, so I just lay on the cold floor and let myself fall asleep. I woke up feeling light and airy, like my whole body was moving through the air. I opened my eyes slowly, not sure if the world would be spinning when I did. Matteo was carrying me to the bed.

"What time is it?" Even my voice sounded raspy.

"It's just after one pm. I tried to get away sooner, but I got stuck in some dumb fucking meeting. Why didn't you call me?"

"Why would I call you?"

"I just found you passed out on the bathroom floor. That's not the kind of thing you ignore and just hope will get better. I'm calling my doctor. He does house calls."

He tucked me into the bed and left the room to make the call while he got me some water. I could hear him from the hallway.

"What the fuck are you doing in Bali? You're supposed to be a private doctor; that means you need to be available, asshole."

There was silence for a few seconds.

"I don't care who got married, I need a fucking doctor. I just found my wife passed out cold on the bathroom floor. I need someone here now, not next week!"

I could hear him angrily throw his phone at the wall and then sigh before coming back in the room, bringing me a glass of water.

"Sip it, love, don't chug." His tone of voice changed drastically between ending the phone call and talking to me.

I was so dehydrated that it was almost impossible not to down the water.

"I'm taking you to the hospital. Do you think you can manage the drive? I'll be there the whole time."

I just nodded. I wanted to argue and say that I could make it, but whatever was making me sick was not going to just disappear in the next 24 hours. And with that, Matteo picked me up bridal style and carried me down to the car. I could barely keep my eyes open; all my energy was focused on not throwing up on the poor man, or in his car.

· ♥ · ♥ · ♥ · ♥ · ♥ ·

The emergency room lights were too bright, and I struggled to keep my eyes open as Matteo walked me inside. I refused to let him carry me into the hospital. There were people there who'd been in serious accidents, and I could still walk (to be honest, I was mostly leaning on him).

As we were sitting in the waiting room, I noticed a mother and her baby. The baby couldn't have been older than a few months. At first, I watched them with my heart warming up. Then, suddenly, a terrifying thought hit me. I had to look away so they wouldn't see me grimace.

It couldn't be! Could it? I almost screamed as the realization hit. I could be pregnant with a Romano child. The thought nearly made me sick all over the waiting room floor. It wasn't that I didn't want to have a baby or that Matteo wouldn't be a good father. In fact, I'd seen him around his family and he was a great son, brother, and uncle. He would make an incredible father. There was no way he'd ever abuse or threaten his kids. I was certain that he'd live or die for any children he would have.

The problem was that I didn't want to bring children into his world. I liked his family, and I'd gotten to know them fairly well over the previous two weeks. They were lovely people who cared deeply about each other and would treat any child like the miracle they were. I wouldn't be worried about my child around them. No, I'd be terrified that someone wanting to get to the Romano family would do so by hurting my child. I'd live with that worry every single day. I would never sleep again in my life. I couldn't live like that, and I didn't want any potential child. I had to live like that.

A nurse came to let me know that it was my turn. Matteo stood up to go in to see the doctor with me.

"I'm going to go in alone. It's easier that way. I don't need you to threaten the doctor." I laughed to make it seem like a joke.

"I want to make sure you're alright."

"No, really. I'm all gross, and I don't want you to see me like that. Let me talk to the doctor, and I'll tell you what they say." I put my hand on his shoulder; that seemed to reassure him.

As soon as the doctor closed the door behind me, I opened my mouth and started begging her to tell me that I wasn't pregnant.

"Have you been having unprotected sex?" She wasn't judging me in the slightest, just needed the facts.

"I'm on the pill and I've been really trying to be strict about it, but I have forgotten to take it in the past. I'm worried I forgot recently."

"What symptoms have you been having?"

"I've spent all day throwing up, and I just realized that I haven't had my period in seven weeks. I usually keep track of my cycle, but I've been...distracted the past few weeks. I didn't even notice until I got to the hospital."

"Well, let's run some tests and see if maybe you just have a stomach bug."

I spent thirty agonizing minutes in the doctor's office while she ran some tests. She took my urine for an instant pregnancy test and my bloods for some further examinations. I sat there trying my best not to freak out. Every time the doctor walked out the room and left the door open for a few seconds, I could see Matteo pacing in the waiting room.

"I'm afraid you don't have a stomach bug."

I looked up at the doctor, my eyes pleading with her to give me some other news.

"You are most definitely pregnant. It's still early days so you do have options if you'd like to discuss them with me."

"No, I want the baby. I just...I just have a few things to sort out. The circumstances are not ideal."

She sat down opposite me with a concerned look. "Is the man out there your partner?"

"Yes." I realized that I hadn't even hesitated. And that scared me.

"Is he hurting you? There are resources available that can help you get out of a bad situation."

"Oh no, not at all. Matteo is amazing. He'd never lift a hand to me or this child. It's just complicated, that's all. I'll sort it out. This has just come as a huge shock, that's all."

When I joined Matteo in the waiting room, I told him that I had a stomach bug and needed to drink lots of fluids and probably get something in my stomach. As soon as we got home, he directed me to his bed, even when I tried to go to my own room. I hadn't slept in my own bed since we'd had dirty sex in his office that first time. He then ordered me some chicken noodle soup and brought me a jug of water and a clean glass.

At some point, I must have drifted off. Every thirty minutes or so, he'd gently wake me up to drink some water and then let me go back to sleep. He continued to attend to me the entire night.

Chapter 16

MATTEO

♥

Arabella started acting strange as soon as we got to the hospital. At first, I believed that I was overreacting. Maybe that's just the way she behaved when she was sick. But she actually looked even paler after speaking to the doctors. I was a little annoyed that she wouldn't let me go to see the doctor with her. I was - according to the rest of the world - her husband and at least deserved to be by her side when she spoke to the doctor. But it seemed important to her that she have some kind of privacy, so I didn't push the matter.

Once she came out of the doctor's office, I thought she'd at least tell me what was wrong, but she kept avoiding saying what it actually was. She just told me that it was a stomach bug and it should be fine in a few days. When I asked what medication the doctor had given her, she just said it wasn't the type of thing that could be treated with medication.

What kind of stomach bug couldn't at least be made a little less painful with some pills to ease the nausea? I was confused, but every question I asked was avoided or answered with a shrug. She seemed really distracted. I would be lying if I wasn't incredibly worried that it was something far more serious than a stomach bug. Why else would she be acting so strange? She was also in that doctor's office for far longer than she should have been if it was nothing more than an average tummy ache.

I didn't push the subject because I could see how sick she was feeling. I decided that the next day we'd have to have a talk. I didn't want any secrets between us, which meant that I would inevitably have to tell her my big secret.

I was in love with her. I didn't want to be fake married anymore. I wanted her in my life full-time and permanently. There were reasons that she didn't want to be with me. But I would figure out a way to take care of it. I would find a way that we could be together because I loved that woman more than I'd loved anyone in my entire life. I would do absolutely anything for her.

· ♥ · ♥ · ♥ · ♥ · ♥ ·

As soon as we got home from the hospital, I set her up in my bed with the TV on and a bunch of movies. She fell asleep almost immediately, but I was there in case she needed me. I couldn't get any rest. I wanted to make sure that if she got sick again, I was there to carry her to the bathroom.

I eventually fell asleep at five am. When I woke up a few hours later, Arabella wasn't lying next to me anymore. I freaked out and rushed to check the bathroom in case she'd passed out on the floor again. But she wasn't there. I ran around the rest of the apartment, trying to find her.

Eventually, I smelled the scent of frying bacon coming from the kitchen. I was very confused. If she was still suffering from a stomach bug, why on earth was she cooking breakfast? Surely, she should be eating bland foods until she's feeling completely better? But then again, I wasn't about to lecture a grown woman.

"Hey, what are you doing up?"

"I'm making breakfast. Just like the doctor said I would, I'm feeling much better. I tried to wait until you woke up, but I kept craving crispy bacon. Do you even like bacon? Shit, I completely forgot to ask you."

She was rambling. Something weird was going on, and I was going to get to the bottom of it. I just needed to bide my time until I sorted a few things out. Once all was taken care of, I would confront her about whatever it was that she was hiding from me. And I'd confess my true feelings to her.

To be honest, if she didn't know how I felt by then, she really should have figured it out. I wasn't exactly acting like I didn't care. In fact, I'd never been so infatuated with a woman before. Then again, maybe she didn't know. I was completely new to all this. And from what I knew, so was she.

Arabella had never had anyone truly care for her without ulterior motives since her mother had passed away. How would she even know what to look for? My heart hurt as I watched her cook breakfast, thinking about all the various ways she'd been hurt by men (and even her sister) over the years. That's not a scar that heals easily.

"Why are you looking at me like that?" She smiled, but there was a hint of concern in her voice.

"I was just thinking about everything you've been through." I wasn't about to lie to her.

"Oh. It's not…people have been through much worse."

I moved around the counter and put my arms around her from behind, placing my lips just above her ear.

"Just because other people have been through much worse doesn't make what happened to you okay. You've been through so much trauma, and, honestly, I wanted to kill your dad when I went to go see him that day. I wanted to end his miserable life. You deserve so much more, and I promise that if you give me a chance, I'll give you everything you've ever wanted."

She went stiff and stepped forward to flip a pancake. I didn't know what all that was about, but I understood that some people who'd been through trauma found it difficult when people started showing them kindness. I decided that I'd ease up and give her a little space.

"So, just like that, you're cured? No more throwing up and passing out on the bathroom floor?" It came out a little more aggressive than I had meant it to, and Arabella gave me a look that told me I was on thin ice with her.

"Do you think I'm lying? How would that work? I'm actually still sick but pretending to be well enough to stand here cooking food? Or I was lying about being sick in the first place. Which one of those are you accusing me of, Matteo? Because the obvious answer is that it was one of those 24-hour bugs that get out of your system in, well, twenty-four hours."

She shoved a plate of bacon, eggs, and pancakes in front of me as though she would much rather have thrown it all over me.

"I'm sorry. Really, I am. I was just so worried yesterday, and I guess I'm still worried. It scared me seeing you in such a vulnerable position. I thought maybe it was something long-term, something big and scary. Not just a bug that you'd get over without medication."

"Well, I'm sorry that my illness wasn't severe enough for you. I'll try harder next time." Her voice was dripping with sarcasm, and I knew that I'd made a huge mistake.

We ate in silence for the next half an hour. Once she'd finished chewing every bite as slowly as she could, I cleared our plates and put the dishes in the dishwasher. I even cleaned up the pots and pans and wiped down the stovetop. I was biding my time, trying to make things right between us.

"I'm sorry. I never meant to insinuate that you weren't being truthful. I just care about you, Arabella, and I want you to feel well and healthy. If that's how you're feeling now, then I'm happy. That's all I want. I hated seeing you not feeling well. All I want is your happiness."

She sighed, and I swear I saw a tear slide down her cheek.

"Thank you, Matteo. I'm sorry, I guess I'm just a little emotional after everything. Yesterday scared me too. I didn't know what to do. But you took care of me; I've never had that before. No one's ever cared enough to look after me when I've been sick before. Thank you for that."

I walked around the kitchen and pulled her into a hug while she was still seated at the counter. I couldn't see her face, but by the way she was breathing, I was pretty sure that she was crying. It broke my heart that no one had ever shown her the kindness of looking after her.

"Why don't we get back in bed, bundle up in blankets, and watch some movies? I'll even let you choose which ones you want to watch the most. I won't even complain if you want to watch Princess Diaries 2."

"Oh please, you loved the first movie, and you'll love the second. You secretly want to watch it, that's why you brought it up."

"You got me there." I was grinning as we walked back to my bedroom.

I decided to just spend the day enjoying Arabella's company instead of trying to explain my feelings. There would be plenty of time to do that. I first needed her to feel comfortable around me and understand that I cared for her before I dropped the bomb that I was completely in love.

We watched Princess Diaries 2, and it did not disappoint. We also watched The Sound of Music, which I'd seen a hundred times growing up because it was one of Mother's favorites. We took naps, ordered lunch at the apartment, and even got through a few episodes of The Vampire Diaries (not to my taste, but Arabella loved showing me her guilty pleasure show).

All-in-all, it was a great day, a relaxing day. It was funny how I could do the most simple things with Arabella, and it would feel significant and important. I had no doubt that I would remember that day for the rest of my life. It would become one of my most cherished memories.

She was important to me. All I had to do was prove it and show her how good we were together. She wasn't happy about my family connections (even though she really loved my family), but she had to know that I wasn't a bad man. I was just involved with some bad things.

As we lay in bed eating popcorn and watching TV, I knew that I would do whatever it took to make her happy. She was the most important person in the world to me. It had happened so quickly that I hadn't had time to really think it over, but it was true. That night, we went to sleep with her curled up in my arms. When I awoke the next morning, the bed was empty.

At first, I didn't think too much about it. I checked the bathroom and the kitchen. She wasn't there. Then I started getting worried and checked the rest of the apartment, calling out her name while I did. She was nowhere to be found. Eventually, I went into her bedroom and started looking through the closets. Half her clothes were missing. Her toothbrush and all her toiletries were gone from the bathroom. Just to make sure, I checked the place where she stored her suitcase, and it was gone as well.

She'd left. After everything, she'd left me. I looked everywhere for a note explaining why, but there was nothing. I tried calling her on repeat, but her phone was switched off. I couldn't believe it: she was gone. And this time, I didn't think I'd find her sleeping on Brian's sofa.

She was trying to escape from me. What I didn't know was why.

Chapter 17

ARABELLA

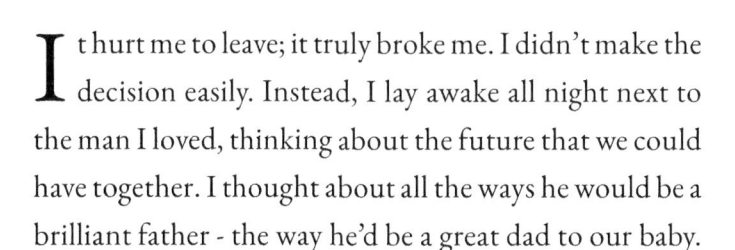

♥

It hurt me to leave; it truly broke me. I didn't make the decision easily. Instead, I lay awake all night next to the man I loved, thinking about the future that we could have together. I thought about all the ways he would be a brilliant father - the way he'd be a great dad to our baby.

The one thing that I could not ignore was that he was also a high up leader in the mafia. He was next in line for the throne. And while I completely trusted that deep down he was a good person, that wasn't enough. He would put our child in danger just because of who he was.

It didn't matter that he would be an excellent father – attentive, kind, and caring. He would still bring his work home. People would be after him because of who he was and his connections. There was no way that he could separate his home life from the family business. If we mattered to him, people would know it, and we'd be in danger.

If it were just me, I might consider it. Hell, I loved being with him; he was an amazing man, one I couldn't imagine leaving. But it wasn't just us anymore. Now, there was a baby involved, and I needed to be a mother first and a woman second. I was making decisions for the two of us, not just me. 'd never put my unborn baby in danger. Not even for true love.

I only had one option: I needed to get away. There was only one person I could think of who would be happy to help m. I hadn't run to her at first because I didn't want to put her in danger. But things had calmed down with the Sullivans, and I didn't think they would leave the country to get to me.

So, while Matteo slept deeply next to me, his arms wrapped tightly around me as though he wanted to keep me all to himself, I decided that I had to leave and take the next flight to Ireland to stay with Grandmother. I would be the first to admit that it wasn't the perfect plan, but it was all I had. I couldn't think of any other alternative.

I knew that I would be breaking Matteo's heart, because I could feel how much that man loved me. But I figured if he just thought that I'd run away because I didn't love him, he wouldn't chase me to another continent. While I knew that he cared, I didn't think he felt strongly enough to search for me. After all, we hadn't even talked about being in a real relationship.

This was all an arrangement until he sorted things out with the Sullivans. I knew he had feelings for me, but he would eventually move on. He was a gorgeous billionaire with a good heart; there were thousands of women out there who would make him happy.

He'd survive me leaving. Sure, he would be upset at first, but I didn't think it would break him. He had a lot going for him, enough that me leaving wouldn't be the end of the world. He would be just fine. He might be sad for a while, but eventually he would move on and find someone who could fit into his world better than I ever could.

He deserved someone who wasn't traumatized and broken from years of being treated like a burden by the people who were supposed to love her. He'd end up with someone whole and healthy who didn't need constant reassurance that she was enough. Someone with a good family and a happy upbringing.

That's what I told myself as I packed the necessities at four am, trying my best to keep as quiet as possible. The last thing I wanted was to wake him and have a giant confrontation before the sun was even out. I would be able to handle the hurt in his eyes if he found out that I was leaving him after everything we had already been through - after all he had done for me over the past few months.

I tried to leave him a note, but I couldn't find the words. How could I tell him that I had a really good reason for leaving but not tell him what that reason was? If he was aware that I was pregnant, he would chase me to the ends of the earth. He wasn't the kind of man who could know that he had a son or daughter out there and not be in their lives.

As I got into the elevator, I heard him start to wake up. He called out my name, his voice gruff with sleep. I almost gave up on my mission and went back to him. It would have been so easy to crawl back into bed and pretend that I was never going to leave in the first place.

Being with him was easy, but leaving was the hardest thing I had ever had to do in my entire life. But I needed to put our child's wellbeing first. I was going to be a mother. That thought made me press the button and close the elevator.

I don't think I breathed the entire descent to the lobby. I didn't trust myself not to go back up and tell him all about the pregnancy. I knew that he would be happy. I didn't doubt that he'd be thrilled to be a father. When I got to the lobby, I told myself that I just needed to put one foot in front of the other, go out the door and into a cab. I felt like everyone was watching. I tried to act like I wasn't breaking apart on the inside. But I was.

Matteo was good friends with all the doormen, so I hoped that they wouldn't call him to find out why I was leaving at the break of dawn with a full suitcase. I crossed my fingers and smiled at everyone I passed like I wasn't running away and this was a planned trip.

I booked a flight in the cab on the way to the airport. I used the money I'd saved up over the past few months after moving in with Matteo. I wasn't paying rent, and he wouldn't let me pay a cent for anything. I was still receiving my paycheck from Gallbury Tech, so I had enough to last me a few months.

Once I was settled at Grandmother's place, I would find a job. I could stay with her and work as a cashier or secretary. I didn't care much, as long as I was able to support myself and my baby and wasn't a burden to anyone.

I was hit with a bout of nausea on the plane and spent a good portion of the time making a run for the toilet. The guy next to me asked if I was a nervous flyer. I just nodded and then turned down his offer of anxiety pills. I didn't exactly feel like explaining my situation to a complete stranger.

I had told Grandmother that I would take a cab from the airport to her place as she had given me the address. Yet, she was at the airport waiting for me as soon as I came out of baggage claim. She beamed the brightest smile I'd ever seen and wrapped me in a huge hug.

I hadn't told her that I was pregnant - just that I needed to get out of New York. She'd been thrilled at the idea of me staying with her. She'd been offering to pay for me to visit for years, but I had turned her down every time, not wanting to be a burden. She was a good person, and I didn't want to take advantage of it.

As she hugged me in that airport, I knew that I could never be a burden to this woman. She loved me and anything she offered to do for me was out of love and not expectation. It was strange, but it reminded me of the way Matteo made me feel - like I was worthy of love just because I existed.

I had never felt like that before.

The first thing Grandmother did was take me to an old Irish pub for food because she said that I looked hungry and she lived two hours away. We needed to stop to fill up. We ate and caught up on the past few years. Even though we talked all the time on the phone, it just felt different in person.

Finally, she stopped and asked me point blank who the father was. I was in shock. I had no idea how she could know. She just smiled and said that she was there for me and the baby. If I didn't want to tell her who the father was, that was okay. It was, after all, my story to tell, and I could decide if she needed to know.

She did want to know if I was in danger if I went back to New York. I honestly told her that the father was a good man and the whole situation was just complicated. In fact, I told her that in another life, if we were different people with different histories, the baby's father and I would be great together.

All she did was nod and give me a hug.

"I'll be here for you as long as you need me. My home is your home; and if you'd like, it can be your baby's home too. You remind me of your mother, and I would do anything for my child and my child's child. You are family and I love you. I'll be there for you no matter what, I promise you. There's nothing you could do that would make me turn my back on you."

That little speech had tears spilling from my eyes. I hadn't been loved that way since my mother had been alive. This was what unconditional love felt like, and it was truly spectacular. I wanted my child to feel that way for their whole life. I wanted them to know that I had their back no matter the situation they fell into. In an ideal world, they'd have their father as well, but we didn't live in a perfect world.

We eventually arrived at Grandmother's house. I almost cried when I walked into the gorgeous place. It immediately felt like home. It definitely wasn't as large and fancy as Matteo's penthouse apartment, but it was even better because it was well loved, and there was evidence of happy memories in every corner.

Grandmother insisted on making me a sandwich even though we'd just eaten an hour ago. She informed me that I was now eating for two and she would be ensuring that

I eat enough. That was her job as a grandmother. I just laughed, tears still in my eyes, and enjoyed the meal.

That night, I unpacked all my things once Grandmother had gone to sleep. I let myself cry as much as I needed to. I wanted to get all the sadness out. I grieved my relationship with Matteo and what could have been. I grieved on behalf of my child, who would never know their amazing father. And I grieved for their father who would never get to know them.

Chapter 18

MATTEO

♥

After I searched the entire penthouse apartment, I diligently went through the rest of the building: the rooftop bar, the ground floor coffee shop, and the five-star restaurant on the 12th floor. I knew deep down that she wouldn't be at any of those places, but I had to try. I didn't want to admit to myself that she'd left me, even with the evidence of all her necessities gone.

After that, I took a shower with the intention of going into the office. It was a weekend, but that didn't mean anything. Maybe she'd gone in to get ahead of some of my work? Again, I knew she wouldn't be there, but I wanted to make sure. I had to eliminate all the options before I did something drastic.

It wasn't unusual for me to go into the Gallbury Tech offices on a weekend, so the security at the front desk wasn't confused to see me there. I asked if my wife had been in, and he slowly shook his head "no". I asked him to please keep that question between us. I didn't need the whole company gossiping because I couldn't find the woman I was married to. I knew he'd keep my secret because when you get to my level, everyone wants to be in your inner circle.

I did a lap around the office and then went into my office and slammed the door. I needed to think clearly. I didn't want to reach out to my father's men for help. Wherever Arabella had gone to, she'd gone out of free will. I wanted to talk to her and find out why she'd left. I didn't want to force her into coming home with me if that's not what she wanted.

I called Brian, and he was of no help. He swore that she hadn't gone to stay with him and even said I could come by and check out his place if I didn't believe in him. He sounded just as worried as I was, saying that he hadn't heard from Arabella since the week before, and he was actually planning on giving her a call.

When I truly thought about it, everything had been fine until she'd gotten sick. Everything changed after the hospital visit. That's got to be where the issue happened. Maybe she was really sick? Maybe it was far more than a simple stomach bug, and she didn't want me to know that she was seriously ill.

I couldn't remember the doctor's name, but I knew that I'd paid upfront for the appointment and tests on my credit card. I called the hospital and asked for the doctor's name as I would like to book a follow-up consultation. They informed me that she was there, and I could come by the hospital to speak to her.

I made my way to the hospital in a hurry; it was only a few blocks over from the office, so I walked...or rather ran. If Arabella was in danger and really sick, I needed to know as soon as possible. I couldn't just let her go without knowing the truth. What would I do when I found her? I'd convince her that no matter how sick she was, that I would be there by her side. I would pay for all her treatments and ensure she got the best medical care in the whole world. I wasn't above flying her to Switzerland for surgery if she needed it. I would make sure that she was taken care of, and I would be right by her side for it all.

There is nothing in this world that I wouldn't do for Arabella Flynn. I would give her every cent I've earned. I would sacrifice everything I had; she's the only thing in my life worth giving up everything for. After I eventually got to the hospital in a sweaty mess, I used my well-known name to get in to see the doctor before the other patients. Yes, I know that was a dick move, but I needed to find out if Arabella was okay and what exactly was happening with her. It's not like there was anyone in the waiting room with a critical wound, as they all seemed okay.

The doctor took me into her office and offered me a seat. But I was too worked up to sit down.

"I need to know why my wife was in here the other day. I brought her in because she was throwing up, and I found her passed out on the bathroom floor; but she told me it was just a stomach bug. I don't believe that for a second. And then she was fine the next morning. What's going on with her?"

"Have you asked her?"

"She doesn't want to tell me. She says that she's fine, but I'm worried about her, doc. I need to know that she's going to be okay."

I was hoping to play on the doctor's sensitivities, but that didn't seem to be working. She just gave me a weird look and shook her head.

"There is literally no way on heaven or earth that I'm going to give you privileged information, Mr. Romano. And yes, I know exactly who you are and the billions you're worth. But that doesn't mean anything. If your wife chooses not to tell you what's going on, I have to trust that there's a reason."

"Please, I'll give you anything, pay you anything. I just have to know."

"No, now please get the hell out of my office before I ask security to escort you out. I have patients out there with real pressing concerns. Just speak to your wife."

I wished that I could just speak to my wife, but she'd cut off all contact, and there was nothing I could do about that. As I was leaving the hospital in a shitty mood, ready to murder someone to find out where the hell my wife was hiding and, more importantly, why she was doing it in the first place, I had a thought. I'd paid for the doctor's visit upfront, which meant that any tests the doctor did would show up on my account.

I backtracked through the hospital entrance and headed to the accounts department. I was just hoping that they were overworked enough to be there on a weekend. I was right, a woman sat there with a pale pink cardigan and a bored-to-death look on her face. I would have to turn on the charm for this one. I walked up to her with that old charmer smile I'd been told made panties melt and tapped on her desk with my knuckles so as not to startle her.

"Hi there, sweetheart," she said with a grin. This woman must have been a little older than my mother.

"Good day, I'm having a little trouble with a payment I made to the hospital. I'm hoping you're the one who can help me out a little."

"Sure thing, what do you want to know?"

"I paid for my wife to get some tests done, and I want to double-check what they are in case I can make a claim with my health insurance."

"Yes, of course, please just give me the date and your account number."

I did exactly that. I paced in front of her desk while she looked up the details. If she noticed my nervous behavior, she didn't say a single thing.

"Oh right, well, there was only one test - a pregnancy test. Are congratulations in order?"

I was so shaken that I didn't bother answering. I just left the building incredibly dazed. Arabella was pregnant. That's why she ran away. But why? I knew without a doubt that I would love that child and protect it with everything I had. She had to know that too. She was probably the one person who knew me better than anyone else. She had to be aware that I'd give up my life for our child.

Then it hit me. She hated that I was part of the Romano family. She'd met my family and gotten along with them really well, but the fact that I was going to be next in line for the throne had never sat well with her. And, after everything she had been through with the Sullivan family, it made sense that she didn't want her child growing up around the mafia.

She'd told me time and time again that she wasn't comfortable with me being so high in the Romano family. Arabella had never hidden that fact. She'd always been honest with me. So, it made sense that when she found out she was pregnant, she would take off.

She didn't want her child to be brought up in a dangerous situation. As a Romano who'd grown up in the family, I knew firsthand how dangerous it could be when your dad is head of the mafia. As great as my parents had been, they'd had to be super cautious to ensure that the children were always protected.

In that moment, I knew exactly where my fake wife had gone to. She'd run away to her grandmother in Ireland. She was the only person who had made Arabella feel unconditionally loved since her mother had passed away. It made perfect sense that she'd chosen her to go to.

I had to stop myself from getting my plane ready for a flight and going to Ireland without even packing a bag. At that point, the reasons why Arabella had left hadn't been addressed. I couldn't promise her that our child would be safe. I could say that I would do anything in the world to protect both of them (and I would mean it), but it didn't mean that nothing would happen.

I had to find a way to ensure that when I went to get her, I had a solution to convince her it was safe to come home. I needed to make it clear that our baby would grow up without any threat of harm. So, I called the very people who made me so dangerous in Arabella's mind. I phoned Dad and my brother and asked them to meet with me. I told them it was urgent and not to bring any of their other men, it needed to be just the three of us.

Within an hour, the three of us were in my apartment. At first, I just listened to Father update me and my brother on family business. The Sullivans were no longer a threat. They had been neutralized and would no longer be stupid enough to come after the Romanos. And they were well aware that Arabella was one of us now, no matter where in the world she was.

Once we had all of that out of the way, I told my brother and Father that I was about to become a father. I explained that Arabella had run away and why she'd done it. They were shocked but understood that being in the mafia wasn't for everyone, especially someone with a history like my wife's.

Finally, I explained my plan to get her back. It wouldn't be easy, but it was doable with their help. That was what I needed from them. My brother was immediately keen on the plan, but Father took some convincing. In the end, we all agreed on what needed to be done.

I started making plans to get my wife back. I just needed to get a few things sorted before I left. I had to be sure that everything was in place. I had to make sure she'd be coming home with me.

Chapter 19

ARABELLA

♥

That first week at Grandmother's was a mixture of both bitter and sweet. It was amazing being around the woman who had always cared so much about me. But, then again, it was incredibly difficult being away from Matteo. I thought about him constantly, even though I did my best to focus on other things.

I had spent all day in the house, just acclimatizing. I was exhausted from a mixture of jet lag and pregnancy. Grandmother didn't mind that I didn't want to go out and do anything. Instead, she made me her famous Irish stew, which only served to remind me of the time I had made it for Matteo. Then she made me countless cups of hot tea while I lay on the sofa and watched mindless television. I didn't feel judged in the least. She even sat with me and commented about how good-looking the boys in Vampire Diaries were, which made me laugh out loud.

Every night, I tossed and turned, trying to get some sleep. It wasn't that the bed wasn't comfortable: it really was a lovely bed. But it wasn't Matteo's bed, and he wasn't lying next to me with his arms wrapped around me. I missed him so much. It killed me that I had left him without a note. I thought that maybe after some time, I would send him an email, explaining that leaving was the best thing I could have done for both of us.

I would need some time before I could do that. Just the thought of being in contact with him made me want to burst into tears. I could tell myself a million times that I was doing what was best, but that didn't change the fact that I missed him and loved him. I thought about what he was doing. I just hoped that I hadn't completely crushed him. I knew that he felt strongly about me. He had never outright said it, but I felt it in the way he treated me.

The next Saturday, Grandmother made me a full breakfast and informed me that I needed some fresh air. She insisted that I go for a walk through the small town. She said the weather would be good for a walk, and I could pick up some groceries while I was out.

I didn't mind because she was absolutely right. If I were going to start a new life, I needed to actually get out and know the town. I couldn't just stay inside in a bubble of misery. It wasn't good for me, and it wasn't good for my baby. I needed to try my best, even when everything inside me hurt as I missed the man I loved.

The walk was actually quite lovely, and it felt really good to get some fresh air. I went to the local market to pick up Grandmother's groceries. I was at the checkout counter when I noticed that a few people were staring at me. I knew that it was a small town and I was new, but it felt really weird.

"You're Laurel's granddaughter, aren't you?" An old man behind me asked with a big smile.

"Yes, yes, I am. Are you a friend of hers?" I put on my best polite smile.

"Yes, your grandfather was my best mate growing up. My wife and your grandmother are still close. Laurel mentioned that you would be staying with her for a while and would be looking for a local job to keep you busy. Is that true?"

"Yes, as soon as I'm settled, I'll start looking online for something suitable."

"What experience do you have?"

"Well, I was a personal assistant back in New York, so I can do receptionist work, secretary work, that sort of thing."

"Excellent!" He was beaming at me. "You can come work for me. I have a small county law firm, and we're in desperate need of a receptionist. I'll write down the address, and you can come in on Monday morning."

I didn't know what to say. It was all so strange. Something like this would never happen in New York.

Hell; it wouldn't even happen in small-town America. But the man seemed sure of his decision and rather pleased with himself. I wasn't about to turn down a job. I still had my savings, but I couldn't risk that running out with a baby on the way. I thanked the man and got his name - Devin O'Leary - and told him that I would see him bright and early on Monday morning.

By the time I got back to Grandmother's house with the groceries, I was feeling a lot more positive about my life choices. It may not have the glitz and glam of New York City and working at a top tech company like Gallbury Tech, but it didn't matter. I hadn't moved to New York because I wanted that lifestyle; I'd moved to get away from my father. And this small town in Ireland was definitely far enough away from my father.

"How was your walk, lovely?" Grandmother asked as soon as I walked in through the front door.

"Well, I just met your friend Devin, and he offered me a job." I had no doubt in my mind that Grandmother had spoken to him about it long before I happened to bump into him at the shop.

"That's perfect. A job will keep you from moping around the house, although I do love having you here, I don't like seeing you so sad. I don't know why exactly you had to leave New York; but as long as you're here, you should at least try and build a life for you and that little one."

I just nodded and smiled. It was strange to be living with a family member who only wanted the best for me. She didn't have any ulterior motives, and that felt amazing. As much as I missed Matteo, at least I was with something who also cared for me and would care for the baby as well.

· ♥ · ♥ · ♥ · ♥ · ♥ ·

On Monday morning, I put on a pencil skirt and white shirt. It was one of the outfits I'd bought to wear to work at Gallbury Tech. I had a feeling that it might be a little out of place in a small town law office, but at least I would try and make a good first impression.

I went and got two take out coffees and some muffins before making my way to the address Devin had given me. I didn't know how many people worked there, so I had only got enough for the two of us. Once I had a proper headcount, I intended to bribe my new coworkers with treats as often as possible.

It was eight am and the front door was still shut. I waited for an hour before I saw Devin walking down the street. He was wearing a pair of jeans with suspenders and a checked shirt. I might be slightly overdressed, but he just smiled at me.

"I should have let you know that we like to start a little later on this side of the ocean. You will find that we're very laid back in this town. Is that coffee for me?"

"Yes, but I'm afraid it's a little cold by now. I'll make sure to bring you a hot cup tomorrow when I know what time we start."

"Oh thank you, dear, but I only drink tea. Haven't had a cup of coffee since I was studying in London in my twenties. Stuff always makes me jittery. Sam, however, loves the stuff so if you want, you can bring her a cup; but she only strolls in at around eleven."

"Who's Sam?"

"She's the other attorney at our little firm. She's a young one, in her late thirties. Came from a top firm in Manchester, but hated working all hours. She came out here to live a little slower. You won't find many people who work less than her, but she's very good at what she does. And, of course, she charms everyone in our little town."

I settled in at my new reception desk, sipping on my cold coffee and eating the muffin I'd brought. The office had a lovely small town charm that I was sure I would eventually get used to, even though I would always miss the fast-paced lifestyle of New York - with the lights, and fast walkers, and generally busy population.

I could get used to a slower way of living, especially with a baby on the way. Of course, I didn't know whether Grandmother had told my new boss that I was expecting. I would eventually have to have that conversation with him, but I had the feeling that he wouldn't see it as a negative.

At eleven am, a woman with bright pink hair and a purple dress barged in through the front doors with a huge cup of coffee in her hand.

"Oh, my God…you must be Arabella! I'm so happy to finally meet you. Laurel's been talking about you since I first moved here. I'm Sam, by the way!" She extended her hand to me.

I took her hand and shook it. "You know my grandmother?"

"Yes, of course. Everyone knows Laurel. Plus, she's in my book club. Or rather, I should say that I'm in her book club. That woman suggests the best reads. You must join us on Thursday. We meet at three pm, but Devin won't mind if you leave a little early. He certainly never gives me any shit, anyway."

I just laughed. This woman was a force to be reckoned with, and I liked her immediately. She seemed so out of place in the small town but also kind of fitted in perfectly. I had no doubt in my mind that she would fit in anywhere she went. She wasn't the kind of person who let other people tell her where she belonged.

The rest of the day went really well. I was surprised at four pm when Devin packed up to go home. Sam had already left. Apparently nobody works past four unless there's something serious going on. That kind of lifestyle would be good when I eventually had my baby. It would make it a lot easier to handle childcare and still be there for the important milestones.

As I pulled into my grandmother's driveway, I noticed another car. I was driving Gran's car, so I wasn't expecting to see one. I thought nothing of it: it was probably just one of her friends visiting. Laurel had a million friends in the small town. But as I walked toward the front door, I had a funny feeling.

I felt him before I saw him. I felt him before I heard his warm chuckle. Sitting at the kitchen counter drinking tea with my grandmother was Matteo Romano. I couldn't believe it. I thought my heart was going to beat out of my chest. I had to fight the urge to run into his arms and kiss him. Instead, I just stood there and took a deep breath.

How much did he know? Was he aware that I was pregnant? Was he mad at me for running away? But then he smiled gently at me and tears started streaming down my face. I couldn't help it. I loved him.

Chapter 20

MATTEO

♥

She looked even more stunning than I remembered. She wasn't showing yet, but there was a definite pink flush on her cheeks; it could have been from pregnancy or just the shock of seeing me. I wanted to get up, pull her into a hug, and never let her go. Instead, I just sat there and watched her take a deep breath. I just smiled. But then she burst into tears, and I couldn't help myself. I sprung up and held her close.

Laurel, who I'd decided was one of my favorite people in the world, silently left to go to her bedroom and give us some privacy.

"I love you. I'm sorry that I never told you before. I should have said the words, but I was scared that you wouldn't take it well. But I couldn't go the rest of my life thinking you didn't know how much I love and value you."

"I love you, too. But there's so much more to this, Matteo. There's so much that you don't know."

"I know about the baby. I know about *our* baby, and I can't wait to be a dad."

"How did you find out? Did the doctor tell you?"

"No, she was very firm about not telling me. But I paid for your appointment, so they allowed me to see the tests. I was certain that you were seriously ill. I was so worried. And then I found out that we're having a kid...and I couldn't fucking be any happier. I swear, Arabella, that I'm going to be a good father. I will do whatever it takes to make sure that our child never goes through any of what you went through with your family."

"I know you'd be a good father, but there is a big reason why I left, Matteo. And you have to respect the decision I've made for our child."

"Sit down, let's talk it through, Arabella, instead of fighting about it. Once you've heard me out, if you still want to stay here, then I will respect the decision. I only ask that you allow me to visit you and our child. I want to be a part of both of your lives, even if you decide to stay here."

She sat down, and I poured her a cup of tea. It was herbal and, apparently, according to her grandmother, good for both the mother and the baby. I wasn't particularly a fan of the herbal taste, preferring coffee, but I sipped it to be polite, anyway. I gave Arabella a moment or two to adjust to having me sitting in her grandmother's house.

"I have a job here." It was the first thing she'd said in what felt like ten minutes.

"I know. Your grandmother told me. She also told me that nobody would be mad if you left. You also have a job back home. In fact, you don't even have to work if you come back. But that's up to you. I'll support you no matter what you want to do."

"I like working."

"Then you can work as much as you like. We'll make sure the little one is taken care of between the two of us. Your dreams are just as important as mine. Whatever you need from me, Arabella, I'll make it happen if you choose to come with me."

"That's not why I left. I left because, as much as I love you and I know that you are a good man, I can't change who you are. You're a Romano and next in line to be the head of the damn mafia. I don't want my child growing up with that kind of threat hanging over their head."

She took a deep breath and then carried on.

"I know you're nothing like my father. I'm certain that you will be an amazing father. And your family is lovely, despite who they are, but I'm worried about what that means for our child. If you're the leader of the Romano family, that means that there's always going to be danger lurking around the corner, no matter how much you try to protect us."

"I would lay down my life for you and our child."

"I know that, but I don't want you to. I don't want your life to be under threat in the first place. I can't handle living like that."

"I knew that you would feel that way. And to be honest, I have never really been interested in taking over as head of the Romano family. That's something my brother has always wanted, not me. I prefer working at Gallbury Tech and making my own way in the world, no matter who my family is."

"But you can't just walk away from your family."

"You're my family. I've spoken to my brother and Father; they've agreed that I can walk away from the family business. According to everyone associated with the mafia, I have paid my way out. I am no longer a part of organized crime in New York City - or anywhere for that matter. It took some work and some under-the-table deals, but the mafia is no longer a part of my life."

"What about your family?"

"They'll always be my family, but only as my parents and siblings. I will have nothing to do with the Romano business. We will never be under threat. I will be nothing more than the CEO of Gallbury Tech and your husband if you'll let me."

"What if I didn't want to go back to New York? What would you do then?" I could tell that she was testing my conviction.

"I would move here in a heartbeat. I can work from my laptop from anywhere. I have more than enough money for us to live a hundred lifetimes if you didn't want me to work. I will literally do anything to make sure that you and our child are in my life. Whatever you want, Arabella, just tell me and it's yours."

"I want you."

And with that, I kissed her. I never wanted to stop, even though I knew that this was only the beginning of our life together.

We stayed in Ireland with Laurel for another two weeks while Arabella helped her boss find a replacement, which wasn't difficult. We took walks and talked about our future. We decided that we would come to Ireland at least twice a year to ensure Laurel got to know her great-grandchild.

We went for the first ultrasound while in Ireland and saw our little bean. I'm not ashamed to admit that I cried when I heard my child's heartbeat. In that moment, I became a father. I was a changed man. I didn't care about anything other than my wife and child's health and happiness.

Chapter 21

EPILOGUE

♥

Eventually, we made our way back to New York City. It was my first time on a private plane; it felt weird because only a few months before, I'd been saving up to see Grandmother. Now I could visit her whenever I wanted. Matteo and I didn't go back to work straightaway. Instead, he took me on a last-minute holiday to Paris. He wanted to show me the world and that was just the start, according to him. He'd been before, so he took me to all his favorite places.

I loved every moment of our trip. We were there for just over a month. On the last night, he took me to a quiet, local French restaurant - it looked like it was in someone's house. Everyone in the place spoke French and seemed surprised to find two Americans there. At the end of the meal, Matteo got down on one knee and proposed. This time, it wasn't for show or to get me out of a dangerous situation.

This time it was for real. He loved me and our child and wanted to spend the rest of his life with us. I cried while he gave me a little speech; the other patrons of the restaurant watched on with confusion written on their faces.

I didn't even hesitate before saying yes. He was my future. My past had been awful, and it was difficult to believe that it was over. But looking into Matteo's eyes, I knew that I would be looked after for the rest of my life because that man loved me more than anything else on earth.

We had a small wedding. It was just the Romanos, Grandmother, and my friend, Brian. I didn't even want my sister there, even though she had tried calling. I wanted nothing to do with my old life. They'd all had their chance to protect me, and they hadn't.

The greatest moment of my life was when I walked down the aisle - hand-in-hand with my grandmother - to see Matteo with tears in his eyes. He had written his own vows, and his hands were shaking as he read them out loud. It was as if we were the only people in the world.

We had an intimate party after war, where nobody drank too much (out of respect for the pregnant bride), and we danced into the night. I loved my new in-laws and what they chose to do was their business, as long as my husband wasn't involved.

A few months later, I gave birth to a gorgeous baby girl. I named her Alicia Laurel Romano, after my mother and grandmother, the two people who had shown me what real love looked like. Because of them, I knew that I deserved the love of a man like Matteo.

I stayed at home for a year with Alicia while Matteo worked part-time, delegating his additional work to a couple of people he'd hired so he could be an involved father. He was as hands on as I would allow. He was there for every feeding, every crying session, every late night and early morning.

Laurel came to visit every three months; when Alicia was a year old, we took her to Ireland for the first time. After we had returned, I went back to school to study counselling to help abused children. I hadn't even thought it was something I could do until I realized that my story wasn't unique. There were so many other children who needed someone to listen to and help them.

Five years later, after I'd graduated and set up my own practice, I found out that I was pregnant with our second child. We ended up having a little boy this time. We named him Matteo Junior. I had to argue with my husband about it. He didn't want it to seem like he'd named his child after himself, but I told him that I wanted my son to be named after the best man I'd ever met.

Eventually, Laurel moved to New York to stay with us as she got a bit older. I loved having her in our home. We moved out of the penthouse into a more family-friendly place on the outskirts of New York, where we could be close to the city but still have a garden and some privacy.

When I looked back on my life, I couldn't believe everything that had happened. It turned out that the scariest thing that had ever happened led to my "happily ever after". When I thought about it, it had all been worth it to get to live with the love of my life.

I had the perfect life, and I couldn't be happier. I had my own family and made sure that my husband and children always knew exactly how much I loved and appreciated them.

Chapter 22

BLURB

♥

He's a billionaire mafia boss with a shady past and now I'm pregnant with his baby!

My dad was never a good man and the men he did business with were even worse.

So when he made a deal to marry me off to the Irish mob, my billionaire boss was the last person I expected to keep me safe.

Matteo Romano, Tech CEO, member of a mafia family and my boss with connections in all the wrong ways.

In order to protect me, I must be his fake wife, which I easily accepted.

I can't seem to get away from this dashing, charming, muscular bad boy.

He surprises me with his sensitivity and kindness hidden beneath his rough exterior.

He soon confesses his love for me and I feel the same.

But how's he going to react when he finds out he's the father of my child?

Printed in Great Britain
by Amazon